PRAISE FOR M. L. BUCHMAN

3x Top 10 Romance of the Year

— ALA BOOKLIST

Tom Clancy fans open to a strong female lead will clamor for more.

— DRONE, PUBLISHERS WEEKLY

(Miranda Chase is) one of the most compelling, addicting, fascinating characters in any genre since the Monk television series.

— DRONE, ERNEST DEMPSEY

(*Drone* is) the best military thriller I've read in a very long time. Love the female characters.

— SHELDON MCARTHUR, FOUNDER OF THE MYSTERY BOOKSTORE, LA

Superb!

— DRONE, BOOKLIST, STARRED REVIEW

A fabulous soaring thriller.

— TAKE OVER AT MIDNIGHT, MIDWEST BOOK REVIEW

Meticulously researched, hard-hitting, and suspenseful.

— PURE HEAT, PUBLISHERS WEEKLY, STARRED REVIEW

The first…of (a) stellar, long-running (military) romantic suspense series.

— THE NIGHT IS MINE, BOOKLIST, THE 20 BEST ROMANTIC SUSPENSE NOVELS: MODERN MASTERPIECES

Expert technical details abound, as do realistic military missions with superb imagery that will have readers feeling as if they are right there in the midst and on the edges of their seats.

— LIGHT UP THE NIGHT, RT REVIEWS, 4 1/2 STARS

Buchman has catapulted his way to the top tier of my favorite authors.

— FRESH FICTION

M L. Buchman's ability to keep the reader right in the middle of the action is amazing.

— LONG AND SHORT REVIEWS

The only thing you'll ask yourself is, "When does the next one come out?"

— WAIT UNTIL MIDNIGHT, ROMANTIC TIMES BOOK REVIEWS, 4 STARS

I knew the books would be good, but I didn't realize how good.

— NIGHT STALKERS SERIES, KIRKUS REVIEWS

# THE COMPLETE FIREBIRDS

A WILDFIRE ROMANCE SHORT STORY COLLECTION

M. L. BUCHMAN

Buchman Bookworks

Copyright 2020 Matthew Lieber Buchman

All stories previously published separately and in other collections. All introductory material is new.

Published by Buchman Bookworks, Inc.

All rights reserved.

This book, or parts thereof, may not be reproduced in any form without permission from the author.

More by this author at: www.mlbuchman.com

Cover images:

Firefighting helicopter © carlosmoura

Romantic couple walking through autumn woodland © alanpoulson

Young men sorting out their relationship © golubovystock

Helicopter on the valley at sunset © Fotolotti

SIGN UP FOR M. L. BUCHMAN'S
NEWSLETTER TODAY

*and receive:*
***Release News***
***Free Short Stories***
***a Free book***

***Do it today. Do it now.***
*http://free-book.mlbuchman.com*

## CONTENTS

*Also by M. L. Buchman*   xi
*Introduction*   xiii

They'd Most Certainly Be Flying   1
For All Their Days   55
When They Just Know   115
They Both Hold the Truth   163
Twice the Heat   225
Last Words   271
Wildfire at Dawn (excerpt)   273

*About the Author*   283
*Also by M. L. Buchman*   284

## Other works by M. L. Buchman: *(\* - also in audio)*

### Thrillers

Dead Chef
*Swap Out!*
*One Chef!*
*Two Chef!*

Miranda Chase
*Drone\**
*Thunderbolt\**
*Condor\**

### Romantic Suspense

Delta Force
*Target Engaged\**
*Heart Strike\**
*Wild Justice\**
*Midnight Trust\**

Firehawks
MAIN FLIGHT
*Pure Heat*
*Full Blaze*
*Hot Point\**
*Flash of Fire\**
*Wild Fire*

SMOKEJUMPERS
*Wildfire at Dawn\**
*Wildfire at Larch Creek\**
*Wildfire on the Skagit\**

The Night Stalkers
MAIN FLIGHT
*The Night Is Mine*
*I Own the Dawn*
*Wait Until Dark*
*Take Over at Midnight*
*Light Up the Night*
*Bring On the Dusk*
*By Break of Day*

AND THE NAVY
*Christmas at Steel Beach*
*Christmas at Peleliu Cove*
WHITE HOUSE HOLIDAY
*Daniel's Christmas\**
*Frank's Independence Day\**
*Peter's Christmas\**
*Zachary's Christmas\**
*Roy's Independence Day\**
*Damien's Christmas\**

5E
*Target of the Heart*
*Target Lock on Love*
*Target of Mine*
*Target of One's Own*

Shadow Force: Psi
*At the Slightest Sound\**
*At the Quietest Word\**

White House Protection Force
*Off the Leash\**
*On Your Mark\**
*In the Weeds\**

### Contemporary Romance

Eagle Cove
*Return to Eagle Cove*
*Recipe for Eagle Cove*
*Longing for Eagle Cove*
*Keepsake for Eagle Cove*

Henderson's Ranch
*Nathan's Big Sky\**
*Big Sky, Loyal Heart\**
*Big Sky Dog Whisperer\**

Love Abroad
*Heart of the Cotswolds: England*
*Path of Love: Cinque Terre, Italy*

## Other works by M. L. Buchman:

### Contemporary Romance (cont)

**Where Dreams**
*Where Dreams are Born*
*Where Dreams Reside*
*Where Dreams Are of Christmas*
*Where Dreams Unfold*
*Where Dreams Are Written*

### Science Fiction / Fantasy

**Deities Anonymous**
*Cookbook from Hell: Reheated*
*Saviors 101*

**Single Titles**
*The Nara Reaction*
*Monk's Maze*
*the Me and Elsie Chronicles*

### Non-Fiction

**Strategies for Success**
*Managing Your Inner Artist/Writer*
*Estate Planning for Authors\**
*Character Voice*
*Narrate and Record Your Own Audiobook\**

## Short Story Series by M. L. Buchman:

### Romantic Suspense

**Delta Force**
*Delta Force*

**Firehawks**
*The Firehawks Lookouts*
*The Firehawks Hotshots*
*The Firebirds*

**The Night Stalkers**
*The Night Stalkers*
*The Night Stalkers 5E*
*The Night Stalkers CSAR*
*The Night Stalkers Wedding Stories*

**US Coast Guard**
*US Coast Guard*

**White House Protection Force**
*White House Protection Force*

### Contemporary Romance

**Eagle Cove**
*Eagle Cove*

**Henderson's Ranch**
*Henderson's Ranch\**

**Where Dreams**
*Where Dreams*

### Thrillers

**Dead Chef**
*Dead Chef*

### Science Fiction / Fantasy

**Deities Anonymous**
*Deities Anonymous*

**Other**
*The Future Night Stalkers*
*Single Titles*

# INTRODUCTION

As an author, I was *done* with the world of heli-borne wildland firefighters.

At least that's what I naively thought.

It had been such a joy to write *Wild Fire*, the fifth novel in the Firehawks series, and *A Hotshot Christmas*, the last of my Firehawks Hotshots short stories. It felt as if it had closed the cycle of discovery that had begun with *Pure Heat*, and Steve Mercer who couldn't stay away from wildfires despite a horrific injury that ended his smokejumping career.

Those final two stories had somehow created a sense of completeness and closure that I found very satisfying as a reader and as a writer. My Delta Force and Henderson's Ranch series beckoned me forward and I moved on.

Further, the flights and fires of Mount Hood Aviation had begun when Emily Beale and Mark Henderson retired from the military in the Night Stalkers series. It had seemed only appropriate for it to end when they retired from the Firehawks and handed off their legacy for a new crew to nurture.

It had been an amazing adventure. Five major novels of romantic suspense firefighters ranging from the Oregon wilderness to Australia, Honduras to North Korea, and finally Vietnam. The Firehawks smokejumper trilogy leapt into fires in Oregon, Alaska, and Washington. For five short stories the Firehawks Hotshots fought fires in and around the mountain resort town of Leavenworth, Washington and the fire Lookouts' five stories told of love atop the high and lonely peaks of Idaho's Bitterroot Wilderness.

Two years passed before I was forced by the characters to revisit this world.

And I do mean, *forced!*

It happens to a writer sometimes. I typically know what stories I want to write next. Many writers don't, but I see my next tales to be told a ways ahead…usually.

Not the Oregon Firebirds.

I had equipped the Firehawks of Mount Hood Aviation with the very best gear. They were well financed and had access to people and equipment of unprecedented quality. Only now, five years after I began writing those stories are the technologies I made available to MHA coming into any regular form of usage.

Then one day, Jana stepped up and plunged into the imaginary chair close by my writing desk. Sometimes characters sit there and point out where I've gone astray ("Oh, I'd never say it that way.") Others just shrug in an amused fashion and say, "Sure, whatever."

That day I hadn't really been paying attention. Instead I was thinking about another story…can't even remember which one. Because once Jana Williams showed up, the rest of it was just gone.

My stories start from characters. And Jana sat there glaring at me, as if challenging me to try and get her story out of her. A wounded veteran, no longer able to fly, trying to find a new beginning.

Beginnings are hard and Jana's was no exception. Broke and broken in so many ways. So many *interesting* ways.

She wasn't just asking me the question, "What happens when a soldier isn't a soldier anymore?" She was also asking the much deeper question of "What happens when a woman doesn't think she's a woman anymore?"

So, I sat down to try and answer her question, but she was slippery. She *really* didn't want to face any of that crap. I mean in a major, former soldier, everything-is-five by five-so-leave-me-the-hell-alone sort of way.

First she had me tell the story of her brother.

That wasn't sufficient avoidance.

So, she shoved the mechanic to the fore next—heck of a stunt to pull on her best friend.

Finally I was able to draw Jana's story out of her. (This may all sound fanciful, but it is actually very close to the real process I went through with these characters—a process I typically can only recognize after the fact.) But once I finally figured out and captured her story, I was too deeply involved with her crew to not finish the rest. The summer assistant was just a summer assistant. Yet he too had a story. One which posed several unique challenges for me—that I'll discuss when we get there—but I didn't see him as ending the series.

No, that final story belonged to a pair of twins. Well,

brothers in spirit if not in fact. They weren't the summer help, they were part of the main crew and were begging for their own story to wrap up the series. They were down with doing that as it stoked their male egos very nicely.

Even that didn't end the way I expected, for reasons I'll discuss after the last story is told.

I have always been fascinated by the women who battle impossible odds. And Jana Williams was definitely one of those. I'm not quite sure why I like her so much, but I do.

I seem to have a fascination with strong women and the choices they're driven to make: Emily Beale (The Night Stalkers, Firehawks, Henderson's Ranch), Kate Stark (Dead Chef Thrillers), Ri (*The Nara Reaction*), and the fireball Delta Force operator Carla Anderson. Miranda Chase in my new thriller series is such a fascinating and complex character that I was forced to name an entire series after her.

What do all of these strong women have in common? Underdog? Perhaps. But my male underdogs don't fascinate me as thoroughly. I strive to write balanced romances—because amazing women deserve equally amazing men—but as the author, it's the women who drive the core of most of the stories for me.

Just like Jana Williams, the founder of the Oregon Firebirds.

# THEY'D MOST CERTAINLY BE FLYING

*The Oregon Firebirds are the very best at one thing—saving homes. Finding their own poses problems.*

***Stacy Richardson*** *flies beside the memory of her brother to honor his past and escape hers.*

***Curt Williams'*** *fears are entirely about the future of his brand new company.*

*He planned for every contingency, except for his sister hiring the captivating Stacy to fly for their Oregon Firebirds. Now a fire burns in more than the trees, it scorches him straight to the heart.*

## INTRODUCTION

Oddly enough, after that entire explanation I just gave about women driving the heart of my stories, this first story was totally driven by the guy.

Curt Williams is just that—a guy. He's not a hero. He's not some warm-hearted, deep thinker with the inner soul of an angel. He's just a good guy.

I don't know if I've ever written someone who was "just a good guy." However, after thinking up that as the challenge to this story (I like to challenge myself), it seemed like the right path to follow. Could I write someone who's just a good guy and make him worthy of one of my heroines...*without* changing him.

He's neither brilliant nor noble. Curt definitely makes his share of mistakes. Even with his best friend Jasper trying to bail him out, he still finds ways to mess it up.

That's okay. While Stacy is an exceptional pilot, she's a bit of a mess in other ways. With reason, but still a mess.

When I start a story, I go looking for interesting

connections. The one for Stacy is a bit obscure, but it gave me a very strong handle on her motivations, if not on her full past.

Her big brother, Bill Richardson, came home in a box after *Take Over at Midnight* (The Night Stalkers #4). The man never spoke. Not naturally silent like Colonel Michael Gibson of Delta Force, he simply never spoke and I didn't know why. Perhaps some part of me knew he was going to die…he didn't get to speak a single word in three-and-three-quarters novels despite being Mark Henderson's copilot for that entire time.

There had to be a reason that a pilot of his caliber never spoke. And it took Stacy to explain it to me six years later. (Yes, a writer's mind—at least this writer's mind—actually works like that.)

Here's the birth of the Oregon Firebirds and the love story between Jana's just-a-guy brother and ever-so-silent Bill Richardson's little sister.

1

"What kind of a heap is that?"

Stacy looked up at the man climbing out of the car next to hers. He'd been riding her bumper since she'd pulled out of Cave Junction, Oregon five miles back. The tighter he'd hung in his black classic Pontiac Firebird Trans Am, the slower she went in her not so classic 1993 Toyota extended cab pickup. They'd barely been crawling when they reached the dusty Illinois Valley Airport parking lot.

He was a big guy—in a multi-muscle way: muscle car, seriously muscled chest under his tight University of Washington Huskies t-shirt, and a total musclehead. His dark wrap-around shades were as retro as his ride.

"My kind of heap. How many miles do you have on that Firebird?"

He grinned down at his car like it was a beloved pet. "Just seventy-five thou. Ain't she sweet?"

"And *she'll* be on the junk heap before a hundred and fifty. Unless," she made a guess, "you replace the engine...*again.*"

He scowled that she'd nailed it. Not hard, as it was a high odds bet that the miles he'd put on it hadn't been easy ones.

"I've already got three-hundred thousand on my *heap's* original engine."

His scowl darkened even more.

Maybe if she waited long enough, he'd move one step closer and she could take him out at the knees with her truck's door. It was low enough on the little half-ton pickup. The truck had been a gift from her big brother, Bill, before he'd been blown up in a "training exercise in Alabama"—except she knew he'd been in Iraq and his death was accompanied by two new medals. They didn't give those kinds of medals for training accidents. It was all she had left of him other than a folded flag and his dog tags.

"What are you doing here, honey? You lost?" The guy asked her in his best demeaning tone.

"What are *you* doing here… Oh, wait. Never mind. I already know."

"What's that?"

"Being an asshole for a living."

Instead of going to fury—she'd quietly put her truck in reverse and was ready to pop the clutch and peel out if necessary—he grinned. "Most folks don't know that about me."

"Seemed pretty damn obvious from where I'm sitting."

He burst out a laugh. It was a big one that seemed to fill the air—which definitely needed something. The April morning was already hot and dry.

The small airport was five miles south of Cave Junction, which wasn't much of a town by anyone's standards except rural Oregon's. Two thousand people and six restaurants—if you counted the Dutch Bros. Coffee drive through—were tucked in the rough terrain close by the California border. The closest town that was any bigger was Grants Pass, over thirty miles back. There was an aridness to the land here that seemed wrong after growing up farther up the coast. Around here, the Douglas firs were scattered rather than growing in thick, mountain-covering expanses. Tall grasses predominated, which would be dangerously dry and brown long before fire season. Even more so around the airport: a flat, baking expanse with no activity beneath the blazing sunshine other than this two-legged laughing hyena.

"Enjoying yourself?"

"Immensely," he was still grinning.

She told herself not to, but was weak and asked, "Why?"

"Because I just figured out who you are."

"You mean other than a pain in the ass." She'd been called that enough times in her life to bury a multitude of lesser sins.

"Yep! Other than that. You're Stacy Richardson and you're here to fly helicopters."

Only one man would know that. Curt Williams—her new boss... Who she'd just called an asshole.

Stacy sighed and climbed out of her truck. At least she was batting her usual average.

2

---

Curt was glad for the dark glasses, so that he could take a moment and really look at the woman. His big sister had sent Stacy his way. Jana was a former heli-pilot for the 101st Airborne and was the logistics arm of their new business, the Oregon Firebirds. She may have lost a hand during a stupid accident while serving in Okinawa, but it didn't diminish her flying smarts a bit.

She'd kicked him a text, "I hired you a pilot. Stacy Richardson is an even better flyer than you."

Women were still rare in the helicopter world, so he'd assumed Stacy was a guy. He wouldn't put it past his sister knowing that for a second. He'd ignore the last part of the message as mere sibling harassment.

Stacy was definitely way better *looking* than he was though. Half a head shorter, trim of waist, but the ranting Donald Duck on her Oregon State University Ducks t-shirt was definitely nicely stretched. She had long dark hair that fell past her shoulders in soft waves tangled by the wind of driving with her window down.

The sun caught red highlights and made her shine. Her aviator shades hid her eyes but not her thoughts.

"Huskies. Oh, my, God! I can't believe that I signed on to work for a Washington Husky fan."

"Beats the Ducks any day."

"And which football team had a twelve-year winning streak over the Huskies? Oh wait, it was the Ducks."

"Which was ended. By the Huskies."

"For the moment. I don't know why you guys even bother showing up. Ducks are gonna wipe the field with you something fierce come fall." And Curt hoped that the second part of Jana's message *was* just exaggeration. Being humbled by a Duck in the air would be a sad state of affairs. Searching for another topic, he looked down at her battered little pickup. The backseat appeared to be crammed with a hodgepodge of belongings. The truck bed had a low cap on it, the same height as the cab. For a moment, it seemed that her whole life was parked right here in front of him just waiting to be discovered.

"You do get that you're going to be flying for the *Firebirds.*" He needed something else to think about because the more he looked at her, the more he saw to like. Good muscle tone, hard-worn running shoes, and an open stance that didn't include the least bit of cowed.

"And your point is?"

With perfect timing, Jasper and a line of the three other pilots who'd be flying with him and Stacy raced into the parking lot. They swooped off the Redwood Highway at high speed, each unleashing a spray of gravel as they slid to a halt: a standard Firebird, a Camaro, and a pair of GTOs. All painted either red, or black with red flames—though none as cool as the Firebird painted on his own black hood.

"What's with the pickup?" Jasper asked as he climbed out of the lead car. "Got us another hot chick mechanic? Way to go, Curt."

"That's my point," Curt told Stacy pointing at the line of cars.

"What? That you hire assholes like you?" But she backed it up with a grin that said she understood he was talking about the cars and was game to take them all on. He could get to like that in the woman.

"Naw," he turned to Jasper and the other guys. "Sis says she's gonna fly the pants off us." He could feel the eyeroll from Stacy at his word choice.

"Sounds like a good contest to me," Jasper tugged on a white cowboy hat.

"Only if you like walking around in just your tighty-whities and a cowboy hat," Stacy shot back at him. She might be a slim-and-trim cutie, but she clearly didn't take shit from anybody and Curt definitely liked that.

"Let's find out," he nodded up the road toward the line of pickups that had followed his crew at a barely more sedate pace.

# 3

Stacy had been flying to fire for various outfits for over five years and knew what to expect from guys.

Cowboy Hat and the other three new arrivals were predictably male, but she was having trouble pegging Curt Williams. One moment he was being true-to-expectations Mr. Macho Jerk, and other moments he appeared to be giving her the benefit of the doubt—which was rare enough in the general male pilot population to be exceptional.

She turned to look up the road where Curt had indicated and spotted a line of three big GMC Denali 3500 pickups with rear dualies. They were serious overkill, but they were very pretty. They could haul far more load than the two helicopters they each had under wraps on a flatbed trailer.

Jana Williams drove the first truck. She was the one who'd taken her up on a test flight over in Bend. She was a sharp contrast to her brother—a serious blonde who kept her thoughts to herself. A man and a woman drove the other two trucks that pulled in to line up on the dirt of the parking area as neat as a line of kites flying from the same string.

Illinois Valley Airport had been the Siskiyou Smokejumper Base and launched teams to fifteen hundred fires from the 1940s through the '80s. Now it was a sleepy, nowhere place without even a restaurant.

"Heart of fire country," Jana had told her during the interview. "And cheap. We like cheap."

There was nothing cheap about the rigs as everyone pitched in to unwrap and assemble the helos. Not only not cheap, but all of it looked factory new. There was serious money behind the outfit, which Jana had proven with the very generous offer that had bought her away from Columbia Helicopters.

The six brilliantly red MD 520N NOTAR helicopters were small, agile craft with impressive power for their size. They were notoriously tough machines, a variant of the ones used by the Night Stalkers her brother had flown for. The NOTAR—short for No Tail Rotor—was a quieter and safer version of the 520. The tail rotor was replaced by a high speed fan to counteract the main rotor's torque. Instead of using a four-blade rear rotor that always seemed to be begging to be taken out by flying debris, the fan simply drove air sideways out of a variable port to counteract the spin. Also, walking into the 520N's low tail wouldn't chop you into little pieces as there were no exposed spinning parts.

Stacy ran her hand over the side of the aircraft. It *was* brand new and completely beautiful.

Just like a military bird, it had her name painted on the side. The Firebirds hadn't merely hired her to fly;

they'd hired her to stay. A bonus that Jana hadn't mentioned.

She looked over at Curt, but he was busy with Jasper swinging out the blades on another helo. The blades had been lashed in line with the tail booms for transport. Somehow she knew that putting the pilots' names on their aircraft had been his doing, not his sister's. Jana didn't strike her as the kind of woman who cared about such niceties—Stacy was surprised to discover that she herself was.

She touched her brother's dog tags where they hung down inside her shirt. They'd soon be flying together just like they had as teens when he'd taught her his own passion for rotorcraft. Their family still had a tourist business flying a helo farther up the coast—a sideline that never did more than break even for her father's farm.

Why any sane person would farm in Otis, Oregon was beyond her. Just because great-granddad had been dumb enough to buy land there using his GI bill money from WWII, didn't mean that they had to stay. It received eight feet, over ninety inches, of rain a year. It ranked eighth in the entire country for days with precipitation. It was a wonder she hadn't drowned as a child. It was also no surprise that both of her parents were alcoholics. Thankfully they were quiet, depressive drunks, but still.

But she'd survived, both the drowning rain and her drowning parents. All thanks to her brother. Bill had taught her how to fly. She'd actually paid for college by flying in the summers. She'd go land near the tourist beaches and put out a banner for sightseeing flights. Dad hadn't cared as long as she took care of fuel and maintenance. It was the only years of success for Richardson helicopters.

Now she didn't know why she'd wasted the time and money. Not the flying, but the college. A degree in political science had seemed practical. Following in her brother's footsteps…until one day his dog tags had come home without him. She'd finished her last semester, though she didn't remember any of it, and then she'd flown. Somewhere in the air over a Montana fire she'd come to—as if she'd spent the last six months asleep. Already doing what she'd been meant to do.

"Gonna just stand there and admire it all day?" Curt had come up beside her without her noticing. His words were teasing, but his tone was kind.

"Thank you for my name," she rubbed a hand over the letters again, barely able to feel the raised surface of the gloss paint.

"It's what a pilot deserves."

She looked up at the wistful tone in his voice.

He tapped one ear, "Mostly deaf on this side. All that kept me from following my sister into the Army. Fine for commercial flying though."

"Bill, my—" but the words choked off on her and she had to look away. She ran her hand over the helicopter's smooth skin again. "Thank you for both of us."

# 4

Curt didn't know what to say to that. There was pain there. And love. He could hear it and it humbled him. He loved his sister, he supposed. Yeah, sure he did. Because brothers loved their sisters, even if they made you batshit crazy half the time just by being alive and drawing breath. But he'd never found anything that would sound like that simple "thank you" did in Stacy Richardson's soft voice.

In silence, he'd helped her roll the helo off the trailer.

They had three of the five rotor blades rigged before the silence built to the point where he couldn't stand it any more. He started babbling about his business plans. He, Jasper, and Jana had worked them out together.

"There's that big outfit up in northern Oregon, Mount Hood Aviation. They fly all these big aircraft, Firehawks and even an Erickson Aircrane. I can loft all six of these 520s for the cost of one of their Firehawks. I could launch ten for the price of their Aircrane. I figure that with the pickup trucks for transport, we can be almost anywhere in the West within a day. And the 520s let us tackle fires in a way that matters to the insurance companies even more than the Forest Service."

"Saving structures."

"Bingo." He liked that Stacy saw it right away. "With a line of six of these little babies, we can get up close and personal with spot fires before they can kill off a structure. We're set up at a discount with the Forest Service so that we get early call to fires and an insurance bonus for every structure we save. Hence the cameras," he pointed underneath. Everything would be videoed and then submitted to insurers as proof for each time they saved a million-dollar home, or a hundred-dollar shed. As far as he knew, it was a first-ever business set up this way and he could only hope that it worked, because he and his sister had gambled everything on it.

They were hocked up to their eyeballs. He hated to do so, but he prayed for a busy fire season. Because if it was a slow one, the Oregon Firebirds weren't likely to see another.

Stacy nodded as if it all made sense to her. More than the financial scheme. As if she could see the dreams and sweat of the last three years putting together the right deals, the right gear, and the right people.

Now why was her approval so important to him? It was like a sigh of relief went through him that it would all somehow work even if smart money said otherwise.

They swung the last blade into place as the fuel truck finished topping up the tank.

She took a moment to glance around the field.

He followed her gaze. Everyone looked ready.

Then she turned to him and smiled. It lit her up.

She was already beautiful, but damn that smile was electric.

"So, shall we see who gets to keep their pants on?"

Suddenly Curt wasn't so sure that he wanted to compete against her in a flight.

Ten hours later, sitting down around the firepit with the other fliers, he knew he'd never risk underestimating her again. After a day of working on shakedowns and team coordination, there was no longer any question about who was the hotshot pilot of the outfit. There wasn't a single guy here who shouldn't be down to his skivvies.

5

"Something bothering you?" Jana asked as the three of them were settling into their bunks after another impossibly long firefight—their fourth major fire in five weeks. It felt good to be back at Illinois Valley Airport even if they'd been on the road more than they'd been here.

The bunkroom wasn't generous; it was best if they didn't all try to get dressed at the same time. Jana had the single bed on one wall. Maggie—their ace mechanic—had the top bunk above Stacy's lower. After the long drive back from the Idaho Trickle Creek Fire, which hadn't been trickling at all, she was too tired to even think.

"Sure," Stacy mumbled. "I'm desperate to know how long we actually get to stretch out on a crappy bunk before the next fire."

"Hey," Maggie stuck out her head and look down at her, temporarily blocking the too bright overhead light that no one had the energy to switch off. The shadows completely hid her expression. "I tightened the springs and put in a new board and everything."

"Sorry. Didn't mean to trigger the perfectionist in the room."

"Look who's talking," Maggie's silhouette rolled back out of sight.

Stacy considered rolling over to get out of the light, but just threw an arm over her face instead.

"We got us a trio of perfectionists in this bunkroom. Now if someone could explain the trash in those other two bunkhouses, that might help some."

"They're men. I guess we need to cut them some slack." Not that they'd been working one minute less than the women on the team.

When they had all first practiced together, it soon became apparent that Jana and Curt had assembled a very skilled group of pilots. But that wasn't enough for them as they'd conceived something grander.

In her experience most outfits debriefed the fire's behavior after each flight. Instead, the Firebirds debriefed aerial tactics. And it was paying off.

On the first fire, a controlled burn over in Corvallis that had run out of control, they'd beaten and battered at the fire. Each MD 520N could deliver a half-ton of water—two hundred gallons—out of the belly tanks rigged between their skids. Curt had even spent the extra for deployable snorkels, so that they didn't have to land to retank, but could just hover over a stream or lake and refill in thirty seconds. If a retardant truck was handy, they could also land and refill in not many seconds more. But they'd made six separate attacks, fighting the fire in too many places at once.

Now, five hard weeks later, they attacked the fire in a

tight line bunched like hydroplanes at the start of a race on Devil's Lake in Lincoln City. They focused on one house at a time. There was no way for their six little helos to stop the main front of a raging wildfire. But first they'd learned how to hold it back around a single house.

Then they'd advanced.

Rather than stopping the fire, they punched holes in it—holes that expanded to gaps. More than once, they'd saved a whole row of houses with the fencelines scorched out between them, but the structures still standing. Ka-ching! That's what they got paid for.

Doing it on their first big fire this week over in Idaho had confused the crap out of the air bosses. They'd had to fight tooth-and-nail to prove that their tactics were saving more homes, even at the cost of more forest. They'd finally convinced that one guy, but the next fire was probably going to be the same battle all over again. It was too exhausting to even think about.

Stacy's body was buzzing with that exhaustion so there was no way she was going to get to sleep.

"I need a beer," not that it would help, but it was better than lying here and not sleeping while her body buzzed.

"Something other than camp food," Jana sighed. "Like…pizza!"

"Men," Maggie groaned from the upper bunk. "We definitely need men."

"We've already got a supply of those," Stacy could feel them in the small huts next door.

"No. Those are our men. We need real ones. The kind we can be stupid about and not regret it in the morning."

There was a sudden silence as Stacy glanced over at Jana.

"Beer," she whispered.

"Pizza," Jana sat up enough to look at her.

"Men," Maggie again leaned out enough to block the light with her head.

"Road trip!" They all said it in unison.

"Shh!" Maggie made the sound far more loudly than they'd been speaking. "Let's sneak. Otherwise our men will follow us and spoil the fun."

Jana dressed in nice slacks and a pretty blouse, a bright scrunchy hanked her long blonde hair into a ponytail.

"You're not going to wear your cosmetic hand?" Stacy had seen it in the drawer, because there was no privacy in a room this small. Come to think of it, she'd never seen Jana wearing anything but the hooks.

"I can drink beer and eat pizza with this one," she flexed a shoulder and clicked the opposing hooks together to emphasize her point. "If a guy can't deal with it, to hell with him."

"To hell with him," Maggie agreed cheerfully and Stacy echoed the sentiment.

Yes, to hell with him, whoever *him* was. Keeping that in mind, Stacy rehung her one fine change of clothes in the tiny closet. Instead she went with her standard Oregon attire: jeans with no char spots, a red t-shirt that said "Fire pilots are like fire, too hot to touch!", and a fleece REI shirt that covered most of the words. She tossed her hair over her shoulder and she was done.

Maggie changed into lacy red underwear—"In case I actually get lucky"—and then a low cut, clingy dress of flirty gold that offset her dark skin so that it looked like she was both glowing and perhaps a little evil. The hem landed well above her knees and pretty much guaranteed her luck if there was a single man anywhere in a dozen miles. She was also pixie high and by far the cutest of the three of them, so she and Jana wouldn't stand a chance until Maggie had her pick. Which was fine, Stacy wanted a beer. She might be tempted by a pizza, but men were nowhere on her list. Not until she found one with an ego smaller than a gray whale migrating up the coast. Not gonna happen on a fire line.

They slipped out the back, climbed into Stacy's little Toyota because they were all sick of riding back from Idaho in the big GMC Denali pickups. Maggie slipped into one of the small backseats that had her sitting sideways and they were off.

Jana turned to the only radio station that reached this far into the hills. They were playing *Boondocks* by Little Big Town. Definitely where they were. They sang along all the way into town.

6

Unable to sleep, Curt had tried to slip out, but Jasper had caught up with him in the parking lot. They'd been hanging together since they were teenagers dreaming of hot cars and chasing girls, or was it chasing cars and dreaming of hot girls. Their moods were so in sync, that it wasn't like he was following—if one went somewhere, of course the other one did as well.

The other three pilots, Drew, Amos, and Palo, were still sacked out.

They'd run into Ty mucking the road trip food wrappers and soda cans out of the trucks. "In case we get a call up tomorrow." He was the camp handyman, cook, and receptionist. Also Jana's right hand in operations as well as helping Maggie with anything that took two people to fix. Ty chose to sack out rather than join them.

He and Jasper had just driven with no real destination in mind. They'd stumbled on Wild River Pizza in Cave Junction and pulled in. He parked his

Trans Am in a shadowed corner so that no one would park next to it and give him a door ding.

They were sitting and watching the local talent, pretty thin on a Thursday night except for some tourists out to visit the Oregon Caves.

"Five weeks. Haven't seen the caves yet."

"Five weeks," Jasper agreed as he tipped his chair back on two legs. "Haven't seen much of anything except fire."

"Good thing," Curt propped his feet on an empty chair across the table.

"Keeping us busy."

"Keeping us paid."

They watched a couple playing pool. There was a nice view as the girl bent over to take a reaching shot. Not bad either when she stood up and did a little happy dance at sinking her ball. The guy standing beside her congratulated her with a kiss that looked very welcome.

"Yep," Jasper observed.

"Yep," Curt agreed. There was such a thing as being too damn busy, even if it was a good thing. The front door banged open and a trio of women strode in. There was a bright light making it hard to see their faces, but the rest of what showed was very fine. Their laughter brightened the sleepy bar.

"Huh," Jasper noted that the prospects for the night had just picked up.

Then the cheery trio stepped past the light and into clear view.

"Huh," Curt slouched down in his seat. Nothing happening, it was the Firebird women. Maggie did look hot, but that wasn't a real surprise—she always abounded with energy, though who knew she had legs like that. And enough deeply bronzed cleavage that…

That… Nothing! She was his mechanic. Besides, he knew that Drew and Amos were both all hot and bothered over her. Definitely didn't want to step into that mess. Still, tonight Maggie was a way hotter and sexier version of herself than he'd even guessed. He couldn't wait to rub it in that Drew and Amos both slept through the whole thing.

Jana too was transformed by dressing up—a major rarity for his sister—and had pulled her hair back. She normally wore it half covering her face. The legs of Jasper's chair thumped down onto the floor. He never spoke to Jana. One of these days, Curt would have to ask what he had against her.

But not tonight, because that's when Stacy stepped clear of his sister.

She looked…perfect.

He couldn't look away from her because she was so wholly unchanged. She was herself right to the core. The only thing she'd altered was wearing her hair down rather than in a ponytail. Damn but the woman had glorious hair.

Jasper tugged his cowboy hat lower until he might have not been able to see them at all.

Curt thought about it, then tugged his red Firebird billed hat lower, but not so low that he couldn't keep at least one eye on Stacy. Moving up to the bar, the women took stools. In moments they had beers and were flirting with the barman.

"Think we can slip away safe?" Jasper whispered from under his hat, though his head was cocked to watch the three women.

"Run or stay?"

"Run. Definitely." All six-three of Jasper was in danger of disappearing completely under his hat.

Best friend said "run," it was probably good advice. He dug out a twenty and was about to toss it on the table when his sister looked into the angled mirror over the bar and glared right at him. After a long moment she mouthed something at him, so distinctly that he couldn't misread it.

# 7

"Chicken," Jana said loudly enough for Stacy to hear but not enough to interrupt Maggie's flirtation with the cute bartender.

"Why? Because I wouldn't answer your question earlier? Fine. Nothing's bothering me that three days of sleep wouldn't fix."

Jana turned to her from contemplating the mirror over the bar. "How long have we known each other?"

"A flight and an interview longer than anyone else in this outfit."

"That means I know you better than any of them."

Stacy considered. Then she raised her beer and clinked the already half empty glass against Jana's mostly full one—way fast for her. "First one I've shared a beer with. Does that make us best friends?"

That earned her a cool look and she wondered if Jana was the sort of woman to have best friends. Stacy liked her well enough—and respected the hell out of her competency—but friends might be a bit of a stretch.

"Beer's talking," she swallowed back some more to

make her point. She'd never had more than two since the day she'd understood that her parents were both alcoholics, never wanted more either, so she was safe.

"I'd say it makes me friend enough to call bullshit on your, 'Nothing's bothering me' pitch."

"But nothing is, other than how good a pilot you are. I've learned more about holes in my technique from you than I think I knew in total before meeting you."

Jana smiled sadly at that. "If I still had my hand, I'd take you up and show you some real 101st Airborne shit."

Stacy had almost stopped seeing the hooks that served Jana as her right hand.

"Anyway, I'm still calling bullshit on you."

"Why?" Stacy couldn't think of anything really bothering her.

Jana just nodded upward.

Stacy went to empty the dregs of her beer as she looked up into the mirror…and almost choked when she saw Curt standing just a step behind her.

8

Maggie had found a couple of retired Navy buddies, traveling with their wives. The five of them were talking Navy jets and RVs. Curt knew from long experience that anything with an engine earned a hundred percent of Maggie's attention no matter how she was dressed.

Jasper and Jana were playing a silent pool game with a grim determination that was actually a little freaky. The remains of a demolished beef, mushroom, and onion large-size pizza was spread across four plates, with a couple slices going over to Maggie.

Stacy sat across the table from him, leaning forward with an intensity that he'd wager wasn't going to make it to the bottom of her second beer. He liked that she was a total lightweight. It fit her far better than a woman who could chug a six-pack. Nervous energy was all that sustained her at the moment.

"What was it like?"

"What was what like?"

She held up a hand and twisted it back and forth in

the air, the fingers curved into a hook. She even pincered her thumb and index finger apart and back together.

"You'd have to ask Jana. She's the one it happened to."

"No, I mean…" Then she grimaced to herself. "I don't know what I mean."

"You mean, you've had too much beer."

"Or too little sleep. Your sister seems to think you're bothering me."

"Me?" He'd been damned careful to steer clear of her. Being around Stacy was like a constant adrenaline high. First he'd been taken by her beauty and sass. Then her piloting—because, damn, this woman could fly. Even his sister had remarked on it. Stacy also appeared to be the first woman friend Jana had chosen in a long time which was rare praise indeed. "How am I bothering you?"

"I don't know. I was thinking maybe you could tell me. I guess we'll never know." She unleashed a tonsil-deep yawn, then her head began sinking toward the last half of her beer and the last slice of pizza.

"Hold on a second." He waved a hand and got Jana's attention over at the pool table. He pointed at Jasper and made a key starting a car motion. Jana asked him something.

Jasper raised his head just enough to glare across the room at him from beneath the brim of his hat. A brief nod—yes, he did have his copy of the Firebird's key with him—then he returned to setting up his shot.

Curt didn't have to carry Stacy out to her truck—quite. Tucking her into the passenger seat almost undid him, though. The first brush of his fingers across her hair as he reached for her seatbelt was the first time he'd ever touched her in any way. *So that's what they mean by soft as silk.* He was careful not to touch her more than necessary as he reached across to buckle her in.

He suddenly couldn't remember if women wore seatbelts under their breasts, between them, or above them. After standing still for a long moment trying to figure it out, he tugged out all of the slack, snapped the buckle into the receiver, then let the retractor pull the seatbelt into the proper place on its own. Between their breasts. Good to know.

She was silent for the entire drive back to the field.

He made a point of releasing her buckle before he climbed out of her truck so that he wouldn't have to reach across her again. To his surprise, when he opened the passenger door, she clambered out. The only light was a distant security light, a sliver of a moon, and the stars.

"You know," she leaned back against her truck. "I think I figured out why you bother me."

"Do tell," he stood in front of her and admired how she looked in the dim light. Soft, real, and still a hundred percent herself. She belonged in her skin like no one he'd ever met. So sure of everything.

"That. Right there."

"What?"

"Well…just look at yourself."

"Hello. It's dark out and I don't have a mirror."

"I don't have one either, Mr. Curt-the-Huskies-fan, but I could describe you with my eyes closed."

"They already are," he teased her even though he could just make out glints of starlight reflections caught by them.

"Feet apart," her voice sounded as dreamy as the night. "Like Paul Bunyan standing in the forest. Arms folded over your chest like a guy on the defense even though he has no reason to be. And I'd wager that you're squinting at me like I've lost my mind."

"Well, you missed that entirely."

"How?"

"My feet are planted so that I don't come any closer. My arms are crossed in an attempt to keep my hands to myself. And my eyes are wide open, because you are a vision in the nighttime. Or in the air. Or—" Shit! He was the one who was supposed to be sober. How had he just said all those things to Stacy Richardson?

"Oh," her voice was almost as soft as the night.

"Oh?"

"Yes, oh."

Now he did squint at her, trying to see her expression, but there wasn't enough light.

"Why?"

"Why? I already told you why." And if this conversation went on any longer he was going to lose his mind.

"No, I mean why are you doing all those things rather than kissing me?"

He looked up at the stars for guidance and didn't find any.

"Maybe that's what's bothering me. You're awfully attractive, Curt Williams, except for your choice in football teams. I'm quite surprised to discover that I like you. And—"

"You're exhausted and you're drunk and I don't take advantage of women in altered states. Besides, I'm your boss."

"I'm tired and I nursed the same half beer for two hours. Probably more sober than you are."

"I'm still your boss. I'm not going to take advantage of you."

"Curious," she tipped her head to the side. "Makes me appreciate that bolt of integrity you wear like a sheriff's badge all the more. What happens if *I* decide to take advantage of *you?*"

Curt blew out a breath in exasperation, "How the hell should I know?"

"Hmm. Let's find out."

## 9

Stacy stepped into his arms—into his *crossed* arms, because she'd gotten that part right in the darkness. She had to rise up on her toes to kiss him due to the additional separation. For a long moment he didn't react...then she felt his smile against her lips. It was only there for a moment, but she found it very encouraging.

"You sure, Stacy?"

In answer she rested her hands on his arms and pulled them down, not releasing his wrists until they were headed around her and she could step the rest of the way against his chest.

Through his sister, he had promised her a challenging job, and he'd delivered. With the amazing quality of the Firebirds' fleet and hiring a mechanic with Maggie's skills, he'd promised safety. And for not being a total guy jerk—actually, not being one at all—*that* swept her feet right out from under her.

Then there was the kiss. His arms slid around her

like they belonged and he eased her in against a chest that felt every bit as wonderful as it looked.

A part of her argued that this was a dumb idea because hadn't she just this evening told her friends that she wasn't interested in any men? Okay, maybe she hadn't told them, but she'd thought it really hard.

For all his macho and firefighter ego, he kissed like a movie-screen lover—long, slow, and perfect. On further testing, he was better than that because he was so impossibly real.

At length she sighed and lay her head on his shoulder as he toyed with her hair.

"You taste incredible."

"Like beer and pizza. I know what a man likes."

His chuckle rippled between them. "Like a dark mystery and the fresh air just rolling in off the wide ocean."

"Keep it up, Husky Boy," Stacy nuzzled in. She could happily go to sleep right here in his arms. "Don't stop and I'll drag you off into the tall grass."

He huffed out a breath against the top of her head like he'd just been sucker punched. It had been a while and she'd forgotten how easy it was to do that to a guy.

She shifted enough to hear his heartbeat and sighed happily. It *was* a perfect place to curl up and disappear.

## 10

"I found Stacy in her bed…alone." Jana found him sitting on the edge of one of the helicopter trailers. "What's up with that, C? Want to talk about it?"

"She fell asleep standing in my arms, J. I carried her in." She'd felt so light yet so substantial. If he'd had a bunk of his own, he might have carried her there. No. No, he wouldn't. But he certainly liked the idea. Maybe he should hurry up fixing the next bunkhouse.

Jana hiked herself up to sit on the trailer beside him. Out of habit, he gave her a hand to provide stability that her hooks didn't offer. That reminded him of Stacy's question.

"What was it like, J? Losing that." He tapped a finger on the plastic socket piece of her prosthetic.

"Seems like a distant dream now. Mostly I remember that it hurt like a son of a bitch. Looking back, I'd say I'm just glad it wasn't my head."

"If it had been, you'd have been fine. You're as hardheaded as I am. But that's not what I mean," Curt almost laughed. It was exactly what Stacy had said, but never clarified. "Guess I'm asking what's it like now?"

He could feel her scowl for a long time before she answered.

"You mean knowing that I'll never be whole again? Knowing that any guy I'd want to take to bed is going to be thoroughly grossed out when faced with a stub of a forearm rather than a hand? Like that?"

"Aww, shit, J." Curt looped an arm around her shoulders and pulled her in.

"That the only guy willing to touch you without judgement is a side hug from your little brother?" Her voice cracked hard and he held her tighter as she cleared her throat a couple times.

"I'm so sorry, J. I didn't realize. We're gonna have to find you a guy who isn't a dope."

"Good luck with that," she was back under tight control and sat up straight. He dropped his hand back to his lap. "Been three years. Why ask now?"

"Stacy asked and I didn't know the answer."

"Huh," Jana didn't sound pleased.

## 11

Stacy focused on the Brookfield Fire. It was a beast that had swept down out of the Ochoco National Forest, destroyed everything along Brookfield Lane in Prineville, Oregon almost before the alarm was sounded. It had already made authorities issue an evacuation order for a whole section of town. A dozen homes were already gone and a new neighborhood was under direct threat.

Assets were pouring in, but they were focused on blocking the heart of the fire that was headed straight for town. The new developments that had been spreading out north and east of the town were wide open. And there wasn't a whole lot of water in the arid countryside. All of the water was pumped out for irrigation of the broad fields, but was little help to their current situation. The nearest open water was the Barnes Butte Reservoir and it was so busy already with tanker aircraft that it was an air traffic control nightmare.

"That reservoir is a five minute round trip away!"

Jasper complained over the Firebirds' private frequency from his MD 520N.

"Well, I'm not real happy about it either," Curt had replied from his own helo.

Most of the swimming pools were shaded by trees that wouldn't allow them to approach close enough without risking catching a rotor. With a rotor disc that swept less than thirty feet, she still couldn't find...

No. There!

"Next neighborhood to the west. I've got two pools with new trees. Maybe we can get in there." She didn't wait for anyone to acknowledge, she twisted her helo into a sharp dive and pulled up hard fifty feet over the first pool. She needed to get down below fifteen feet to dip her dangling snorkel hose into the water—ten was better. That would place her main rotor at seventeen feet above the ground.

There was one tree that was just too tall and close to the pool. It would be too risky to catch her tail rotor. Wait. This was a NOTAR helicopter. Having no tail rotor hadn't mattered at any time in the prior firefights, but her tailboom stuck six feet past the edge of the main rotor disc—so, unlike a conventional tail rotor, the NOTAR's tail could brush the trees and her main rotor would be safely in the clear.

The only problem was that she couldn't see it because it was directly behind her.

"Curt, spot my tail boom."

"You gotta kidding me."

Stacy wasn't, so she began settling down toward the swimming pool as Curt called distances. She liked his voice in her ears, like when he'd whispered in her ear at night.

They'd woken to a fire call the next day after their first kiss. But he hadn't protested when she'd dragged him into her tent that night. He was as self-assured a lover as he was a pilot. And every bit of that ego was deserved—he was the best lover she'd ever had and Stacy did her best to return the same.

"Fifteen feet," he called over the radio from where he hovered to one side for a clear view.

Thoughtful, considerate, and with a body that a woman could gladly wear herself out getting to know. They'd been cohabiting for a month, often too tired to do more than collapse together, but the nights they were awake for more were notably spectacular. There'd been the night camped along a remote curve in the wilderness along the Rogue River.

"Ten."

She continued easing down and released the snorkel. She leaned her head out into the bubble window mounted in the pilot's side door. The acrylic was bowed outward so that she could look directly down.

"Still ten."

That's how she rated Curt as well. A month together and still a ten. Unheard of in her experience. Last week they had flown into one of the hundreds of coves along the Oregon Coast only accessible by boat or helicopter. For two glorious days they hadn't even bothered with clothes, making love on the pale sand with only seagulls, sandpipers, and a rather curious seal out in the surf looking on. A powerful man's naked body lit only by a beach campfire as he'd grilled salmon had been a revelation.

"Five. I don't like this, Stacy."

But he wasn't calling her off yet and she continued

descending. She spied along the snorkel and shifted closer to the edge of the pool away from the trees. Her rotor's downwash blew aside lawn furniture and scattered pool tools. The owner, who should already have evacuated, stood on his rear deck yelling at her and shaking his fist. He was more worried about the neatness of his lawn than the fast approaching wildfire.

"Back up to eight with that last move."

The way they moved together was pure magic. Their bodies finding rhythms that echoed far deeper than merely a happy nervous system. The synchronicity was tighter than between an intermeshing rotor system. Except she had no tail rotor. It should be disorienting. Instead, she felt clearer than she ever had before in her life.

The snorkel hit the water five feet from the pool's edge, she eased forward another three feet. The owner had retreated to glower through his sliding glass door.

"Ten or eleven," Curt called out.

Stacy hit the pump switch and the belly tank that hung between her skids began filling.

"Okay, listen up. My alignment points are the swim ladder exactly bracketing a gate in the fence. That will give us ten feet of tail clearance. We're less than a thirty-second flight from the fire. That means that three of us can work this pool. Come in, load up, fly out to deliver as the next one round-robins down to fill. See if we can do that at the other pool."

"On it," Jasper called just as her tank hit full and she eased up and out.

Damn but she loved flying these aircraft. The Firebirds totally rocked.

12

Curt came dropping in close behind her. Amos hovered in turn and began calling Curt's tail clearances—they stayed above ten feet the whole way using Stacy's guideposts.

Within minutes they had two three-helicopter rotations gulping up and delivering two hundred-gallon loads of water in a near continuous stream. That was as fast as most fire trucks could deliver it—except the trucks had already been ordered to fall back a street and were no longer on the front line.

One by one they chopped gaps in the fire with their helos—down to the pool, pump, up even as Amos' bird came down, follow Stacy to the fire, dump on the burning trees and lawn, turn back to pool, down as she once more lifted away. They herded the flames through vacant lots where the firefighters on the ground had set up wet lines and were pumping for all they were worth.

It was like a dream, following in Stacy's wake. That's how it felt being with her. He'd always thought of himself as the leader type—the Firebirds had been his initial idea. But he couldn't keep up with Stacy. In the air, she was magnificent, and on the ground… His body was still tingling with the memory of her running wild on the beach. She'd raced laps along the wet sand which stretched a half mile end-to-end, dressed in only a sports bra, sunglasses, and tennis shoes. Like a goddess Venus in dog tags risen from the waves for his own private delight.

She never spoke about those dog tags, even though they'd often been the only thing she wore. He'd read the name. She'd lost a husband in one of the wars. That had to be some bad pain and he was careful not to bring it up.

The pools were running dry by the time they had this section of the fire beaten without a single house lost. Though Curt was glad he wouldn't have to face the owner of the empty pool—he was still giving them a dirty look out the back window every time he tanked up.

"Refuel," he ordered the team. Hover-and-lift burned the Jet Fuel A fast. And with a whole neighborhood secured it was time for them to get down and take a break as well.

Jana had a helispot set up at a scenic viewpoint on the far side of town, just a few minutes' flight away.

Once more he was following Stacy like a hungry dog who couldn't get enough. And he knew he never would, not given a dozen years to try, or a hundred.

There was a startling thought. A lifetime? Could he have found his lifetime lady? He'd never really expected to. Oh, he'd find someone to settle down with someday, but there wasn't time in his life to do the finding. He was maxed out with keeping the business afloat. They were doing well, but the season was far from break-even still.

An early end to the fire season could still kill them off far too easily.

He didn't want the distraction of a relationship. It didn't matter that she made him feel smarter, stronger, better than he knew he was. A relationship right now would be a pain in the ass.

That had him chuckling to himself as he settled down in Ochoco Wayside State Park just north of a bright green golf course, so well irrigated that there wasn't a chance of it burning. The wayside was a parched area of browning grasses and thirty-foot Douglas fir and larch scattered about. But the viewpoint itself was a paved loop with enough room to safely land their six Firebirds. Jana had parked the service and transport vehicles along the entry road and set up camp while they'd been fighting the fire.

Pain in the ass. That's how Stacy Richardson had introduced herself. The only pain she gave him was when they weren't side by side.

He fell in beside her as they crossed over to where the ground team had set up a lunch spread for the pilots.

"You're gonna marry me when this is all over, right?" He tried to make it sound like a joke at the end, because he sure as hell hadn't meant to say it from the beginning. Marriage? Shit, no!

"Sure," he was glad her tone was light—lighter than his. "Just as soon I can think of any reason that I'd want to."

Curt grabbed her hand to stop her. She looked at him in surprise, but he held his silence until the other pilots had moved by them at Cruise Speed (max) toward the picnic table.

"There's going to be a reason, isn't there?" He

asked as soon as they were alone. He hadn't meant to sound so serious—was surprised to discover that he was.

She reached out and brushed a thumb down his cheek.

Turning his head into her hand he was able to leave a kiss in her palm.

"Been practicing that romantic approach for a while, have you?" Her smile said that she knew he'd blurted it out without intending to.

"I…know how to fly." How to deal with the woman looking up at him with those warm brown eyes was beyond him.

Then he saw a hint of sadness in her eyes and he didn't like where that was leading at all. He wanted to turn his good ear toward her and ask again because he couldn't be hearing this properly…but there was nothing wrong with his vision.

She brushed her thumb down his cheek again, then followed the others to the table.

Jana was headed the other way to join Maggie in checking over the helos and making sure they were ready to go aloft again. His sister had cooled toward Stacy at the same rate that he'd been heating up. His sister was the best judge of people he'd ever met, but she was wrong this time.

"Trouble in paradise, C?" Jana said as she passed him.

"Eat hot shit, J!"

She stumbled to a halt and turned back to look at him. "Rattlesnake bite you?"

He glared at her.

"Look, Curt," it was never a good sign when she

used his full name. "I've got some issues with her, but they're mine. Don't let them affect you."

"What issues? She's amazing."

"In bed, I'm sure." Jana grimaced an apology. "There's something hidden in her and I don't trust it. She's damaged goods and I know what I'm talking about." She raised her hooks to emphasize her point.

He'd forgotten about the night Stacy had asked him about Jana's artificial hand. It had been a strange thing to do and he remembered it gut-punching his sister when he'd related the story later that night.

"She ever mention it?" he asked, nodding toward her hand.

"Not a word, not a glance. You two have been shacking up, so I only see her on the flight line or at meals, but there's something about it that bothers her in a weird way."

At his silence, Jana shrugged and moved off.

Curt knew he wasn't the deepest thinker, but Jana's caution had kicked him into high gear—or at least a higher one than usual. Jana's radar about people was always spot on. His was okay with guys, but lousy with women.

Was Stacy backing away because he had a handicapped sister? That didn't sound right. If it wasn't that, he didn't know what it could be. He could try asking, but some part of that higher thinking gear warned him that he might not like the answer—like probing a sore tooth until it was screaming.

13

Stacy couldn't believe it. How could something so good become so screwed up in a single week? By the time they left the fire in Prineville, Curt had been growing distant. Jasper, of course, picked up on it right away and began avoiding her as well. Between one moment and the next, she'd become the rotting jellyfish on the beach.

Back at their Illinois Valley Airport base, the nerves had caught up with her in the middle of the night. She'd slipped out of Curt's bed and headed out into the dark. She couldn't exactly move back in with the girls—Jana had made it clear that she wanted nothing to do with her.

At a loss for where else to go, she climbed into the back of her pickup, leaving the cap's tail flap up so that she could see the stars.

It was too familiar. Too real.

She and her brother had camped together in this truck—a lot. They'd had to leave the tailgate down, even in the rain, because Bill's legs had been too long for the short bed. They'd scrunch up together, pressed shoulder-to-shoulder by the wheel wells intruding from either side and tell stories and make up jokes. After he'd joined the Army, they'd spent almost all of his leaves out camping. Then he'd told her everything he could about flight operations.

Now she huddled alone in the dark, lying on the truck bed, clutching her fist around the dog tags that were the most prized vestiges of Bill's life: the last thing to have touched him that she had. The dog tags that Curt had never asked about. There was no going home. If she went back to the family farm, she'd never leave.

Instead, she'd rot there just like her parents and never—

"He throw you out?"

Stacy yelped in surprise at hearing Jana's voice echo inside the truck's cap. She could make out Jana's silhouette where she'd leaned her crossed arms on the tailgate.

"Sorry to have spooked you."

"You don't sound it."

The shadow shrugged.

"No, I left on my own. He was sleeping."

It earned her a Williams family trademark grunt.

"I thought you weren't talking to me."

Again the shrug. "You've got him pretty screwed up. Figured I'd ask why. You having fun doing that to my brother?"

"No!" It burst out of her without thought or pretense. "I am?" She hated how that felt.

There was an odd sound that Stacy couldn't figure out at first. Like someone tapping their fingers together…if they were made of steel and rubber.

"I don't intend to be. But I can't marry him."

"Marriage?" Now it was Jana's turn for an outburst. "My idiot brother proposed to you?"

"Sort of… Not really. But maybe…"

"When?"

"The day of the fire in Prineville, after we did the swimming pool trick."

"I reviewed the footage on that. That was some ace work. Really first-skill flight."

"Thanks. I guess."

"Do you mind?" Then without waiting for an answer, Jana lowered the tailgate and sat down on it.

Not wanting to talk to Jana's back, Stacy scooted forward until they were sitting side by side, dangling their feet off the end as if neither of them was willing to jump into the swimming hole.

Jana was the first to break the silence. "Why did you want to know what it was like to lose my hand?"

"I didn't. Don't. It must have been awful."

"My asshole brother says you did."

"No, I…" Stacy had the nasty feeling that she was finished with this outfit. For a brief moment in time, she'd thought she'd found somewhere to be. Flying to fire, in a helicopter with her very own name on it, an amazing lover, but… "I wanted to know what it was like *for him* to almost lose his sister. I shouldn't have asked."

"Why did you?"

Stacy tried to think about how to not answer that question, but wasn't having much luck. Jana was in her scary-interviewer mode and it was definitely working.

"This truck belonged to my brother. He was all that saved me from my life. From my past."

"But you have it now."

"But I have it now. He flew for the Night Stalkers."

That earned her a low whistle of respect. "Where is he now?"

"In an urn of ash buried beneath a cross at Arlington Cemetery. Better than Otis, I suppose."

Jana's silence let Stacy slowly tell the rest of the story about home, and flying, even her foolish dreams of flying with her brother in the Army someday.

"I couldn't face the Army after he died. So, I flew to fire instead. Swore I'd never marry a pilot. Curt slipped past my guard. I wasn't even aware of it until he made that joke about marriage. Then I knew that I had no choice. I love flying with the Firebirds and my brother taught me to fly an MD 500, so the 520 is like coming home. But I can't marry a pilot."

Jana was silent for so long that Stacy was starting to wonder if she'd ever speak to her again. There was enough time for most of Orion's belt to move from one side of a treetop to another.

"Jana?"

"I'm just trying to decide which of the three of us is stupidest here."

"Stupid?"

"Maybe thoughtless is a better word."

"I'm not a big fan of either one."

"Doesn't surprise me, Stacy. That's one of the things I liked about you in that first interview. Smart woman who was on her toes. The thing is, I think we've all screwed up in this case."

"Might as well tell me, because I can't feel any worse at the moment."

"Me first." Jana tapped her hooks on the tailgate loudly enough to startle Stacy. "Because I thought you were being typically ghoulish about my amputation, I dumped you into my not-worth-wasting-my-time-with pile. The fact that you started screwing my brother the next night just confirmed that you were a first-class bitch."

"Usually I'm called a pain in the ass. And I started *screwing* him, because he's the nicest and best man I've ever met."

"Was that opinion before or after he took you to bed? No, don't answer. If you were in the running, you'd never make more than second-class bitch in this outfit, because I'm gonna win that first prize any day of the week."

Stacy found herself smiling at Jana's dry tone. It felt more like that night they'd sung songs together on the way to the Cave Junction pizza joint.

"My brother—who I love dearly, don't get me wrong—is about as deep as a mud puddle. He's a good guy, but if you're going to marry him, just accept that if you want him to know something, you're gonna have to tell him. Directly, in simple words. He'll never think to ask."

"But I'm not—"

"Number Three of this screwed up trio is you. Why the hell *wouldn't* you want to marry a heli-pilot? Nobody else is ever going to meet our standards. We're heli-women of the Firebirds. There's nothing better than us and we deserve the same."

Stacy didn't know what to say to that. Had she somehow had it backwards all this time? Her brother had been a helicopter pilot, and he was the best man she'd ever known.

And Curt? After such a short time together, Curt was already at a tie with Bill in her heart. What would he be with more time? Would he be even more than she thought he was? Even better than he already…

She ran out of steam. Sitting here on the back of her brother's old truck—less than a hundred feet from the bed she'd left Curt in—and she missed him like he was a thousand miles away. Curt Williams wasn't a part of her thoughts, he was a part of her very breath.

"Hey."

Stacy startled. Curt was standing only a few steps in front of her. She turned, but Jana was gone and Stacy didn't know for how long. Long enough for Orion to move fully clear of the treetop and for Canis Major, his loyal dog, to start the transition.

"Hey yourself." *Brilliant response, Stacy.*

"I woke up and I missed you."

"You found me." She hoped that it was a good sign that he even wanted to.

"Let me guess. You're sitting here in the middle of the night, thinking about how to tell me you're going to finally upgrade this old thing for a nice new Chevy Camaro ZL1."

Jana was right. Curt Williams was a very straight-ahead guy, but he was also such a good one. To offer a tease despite everything else that had happened between them these last days. She couldn't imagine finding anyone better. Ever.

"If I ever do, I'm having it painted Oregon Duck green and yellow."

"You wouldn't!" he sounded aghast.

Then, in a very different tone. One full of the night and just the two of them, he asked softly.

"You okay?"

She reached out and found his hand, then tugged

him toward her. Stacy pulled him in until she lay her ear on his heart and wrapped her arms around his waist.

Slowly, ever so slowly, he wrapped his arms around her in answer.

Yes, she was okay. With Curt to ground her and keep her sane, she could finally be okay.

But for him? Then she smiled and turned her nose into his sternum. He'd already made his choice. Next time he gave voice to it, she wouldn't be stupid or thoughtless. Neither would she hesitate. Though there wasn't a chance he was going to make her trade in her pickup on a muscle car.

Other than that, for as long as they were together, they'd most certainly be flying.

# FOR ALL THEIR DAYS

***Maggie Torres, helicopter mechanic,*** *respects two things: her US Coast Guard mechanic father, and a sweet-running turbine engine. As for men? She can't find one who sees the person behind the hot Latina. Never mind one who revs her own engine.*

***Palo Akana*** *flies to fire. But he hides a past that he knows can never meet Maggie's standards. It's when the two of them collide that the sparks really begin to fly.*

# INTRODUCTION

Maggie is a hoot. There's no question who is in control of her story...it's her all the way and menfolk had best beware.

I've written a couple of go-getter Latinas before—most notably Sofia Forteza in *Wild Justice* (Delta Force #3) and Alejandra in *Love's Second Chance* (Delta Force short stories #5).

But I set two challenges for Maggie Torres. The first one was a surprise for both of us—she's a Latina from... Oregon. Who woulda thought? However, it does make a great deal of sense. There is a large Mexican immigrant population in the state. They were initially drawn there as workers for the massively productive Willamette Valley farms. They stayed for the country's most significant wine region after Napa Valley and were (and are) a large contribution to the state's success. Now they are fully integrated in all levels of the community.

But I wanted her to be dug in—a long-term resident—not a recent immigrant. So, I moved her to Astoria, Oregon. It's one of the largest US Coast Guard bases on the West Coast. The mighty Columbia River reaches the Pacific here, carrying an immense amount of trade over some of the most dangerous waters in the world. It was there that her father taught her the love of a well-maintained aircraft.

The other types of love proved more elusive.

The second challenge I had with Maggie was that I wanted to discover what lay beneath that easy confidence. From the outside, Latina women I've known always have this impossible confidence. Even if they don't, it still seems to radiate off them.

In the first story, *They'd Most Certainly Be Flying*, Maggie had her act supremely together. But what if it wasn't?

If she wasn't who she seemed to be, it seemed only fair that her hero wasn't either. And hence was born a fun romance with some layers of interest that I don't think I've faced before in a short story.

I just hope I made them happy for *All Their Days*.

1

"Moon eyes," Stacy whispered.

"I tell you what I'm gonna do," Maggie didn't even bother turning around. "This *chiquita* is going to poke out the eyes of those two *niños pequeños* and feed them to the pigeons." Being a Latina woman from Astoria, Oregon meant she didn't pull out her Spanish very often, but these *little boys* were getting irritating.

"Too bad there aren't any pigeons around here."

"Why you gotta spoil a girl's fun, huh? Just because you got Curt to put that pretty ring on your finger?" Maggie traded a grin with the Firebirds' Number One pilot.

"Yep. Must be why I do it." Stacy's voice went all dreamy in a way that no man was ever going to hear from Maggie Torres' lips.

She dug around in her toolbox until she found a nice thirty-inch long crowbar, nearly half as long as she was. "They still there?"

Stacy made a show of moving to check something in

the MD 520N helicopter's cockpit, not that anything there mattered until Maggie finished servicing the engine.

"Uh-huh. About ten feet off your six."

It was cracking ninety today in the southwest corner of Oregon at the Illinois Valley Airport and the midday heat had her stripped down to a tank top and gym shorts while she worked. So of course the guys were watching the show when they were supposed to be cleaning out the trucks from the last wildland firefight.

She raised the crowbar as if to tap something on the engine that was out of her reach. Then she spun and swung her arm down. The eight pounds of steel spun through the air for one full turn, then spiked down to punch a hole in the dirt between Amos' and Drew's sneakers—which were maybe a foot apart. Both pilots yelped and scattered.

The bright flush on their cheeks as they went back to work told her they weren't even aware of staring. Two nice boys stuck in the middle of nowhere caught daydreaming about pretty women. Well, she didn't want no "nice" boy. She wanted someone who fired her blood like the inlet temperature of the 520N's Rolls-Royce 250 turboshaft engine—eighteen hundred degrees of pure heat.

"They're never going to stop, Maggie. They don't even know they're doing it," Stacy confirmed Maggie's own assessment as she yanked the crowbar out of the dirt, stalked back, and dropped it into the toolbox. "You're the prettiest woman for probably ten miles around. You make men's brains switch off."

"We're in the middle of the Siskiyou Mountains, probably a hundred miles."

"Two hundred," Stacy agreed.

"Now that might be bragging. Besides, I remember seeing *some* girl in a wedding dress recently who looked pretty damn hot."

"I did, didn't I? Killer dress you helped me pick out. Curt certainly seemed to think so."

"The man couldn't even speak," Maggie remembered his stunned puppy look. Maybe on the right man, Maggie wouldn't mind that look so much.

"Might not have spoken much, but he had plenty to 'say' when he took it off me."

It was one of the best parts of working for the Firebirds. Maggie loved the six machines she'd been hired to take care of. Loved watching the team of MD 520Ns fly to the firefight. But she also was getting seriously used to having a girlfriend in the outfit. She knew how she looked and that it had a way of pushing other women away.

Not Stacy. They'd hit it off early and solid, like a well-tuned V8 engine.

Jana Williams, the outfit's co-owner with Stacy's new husband was a little daunting, but she'd been that way when they'd both been in the Army. She and Jana hadn't overlapped much, mechanic and pilot, but Jana had given her such a sweet offer that she'd signed on with the Firebirds rather than another tour with the Army. While it might not be deep friendship, it counted for a whole lot.

Amos and Drew, however, were being a major pain in her ass—almost literally. She'd seen it the moment they crawled out of their matching black GTOs with red flames painted down the sides at the start of the season. They weren't bad guys. They just turned into moon-eyed stunned puppies whenever they got around her.

She snatched up a 12mm wrench and began checking the tightness of all of the hydraulic fittings while Stacy inspected the air filters, using compressed air to blow out any built-up fire ash. There were some tasks Maggie would let a pilot do, mainly because there was no way for them to screw it up.

"I want my man to be made of stuff better than…man."

"I don't know," Stacy moved on to checking the control linkages from the cyclic and collective controls to the rotor head.

Maggie had already done those, so it was a safe task. She wouldn't have let Stacy even do things like that, except she really *was* a good mechanic by anyone else's standards other than Papa or Maggie herself. Her father had serviced Coast Guard helos for thirty years; he still did. He'd started teaching her how to wrench a helo before she'd started kindergarten. Two tours in the Army, she'd had to put up with a ton of exactly the kind of shit Amos and Drew were doing. Two "macho" guys who couldn't figure out how to even speak to her.

"I like the stuff that Curt is made of," Stacy was doing more of that dreamy thing.

"That's 'cause you just got married, bitch, and like showing off. You don't got to be fishing around in the barrel like the rest of us poor *chicas.*"

"Nope," Stacy sounded far too happy about that fact.

But Maggie couldn't think of what to say back. Stacy was an awesome pilot, even Jana said so which meant something serious. She was totally nice, like girl-next-door nice. Maggie had always liked her three sisters, but they'd stab you in the back and steal your boyfriend faster than you could change your shoes if you let them. Stacy wasn't like that. She also was walking as if her feet weren't going to ever touch the ground again, which was just showing off to Maggie's way of thinking.

She sighed. Except for occasional fishing trips to the couple of bars in Cave Junction, it was going to be a long, dry summer. On the fire line, the firefighters usually just collapsed into exhaustion when they came off the line—not as if she had spare time and energy during a big fire herself.

Hydraulics were all tight. She began greasing the linkages to the rotorhead and NOTAR fan.

## 2

"Heading up," Curt called over the radio on the Firebirds' private frequency. The fire commander's frequency was set to just monitor.

"Roger that." Palo waited until Curt was aloft and far enough clear for the air turbulence to settle, before easing up on his own MD 520N's collective. With a full load of two hundred gallons of water aboard, he'd take the clearest air he could find to get lift.

There were just three of them fighting a small fire in the hills southeast of Depoe Bay along the Oregon Coast. He'd never imagined this section of the Oregon forest could *get* dry enough to burn. Some idiot hikers' campfire, sparking off after they were long gone because they didn't know how to douse it properly. It gave them work, he supposed. Department of Forestry would normally let something like this burn quietly to clear out the undergrowth, but the wind was sliding out of the northwest for a change and driving it toward the town of Siletz.

Not big enough to call out the full flight of six helos,

they'd loaded up just three of the six Firebirds and headed over to kill it off before it got out of hand.

Jasper followed him aloft as silently as ever.

There weren't any natural firebreaks between Depoe Bay and Siletz, but a team of hotshots were on the ground making one out of an old logging road. The Firebirds' assignment was to narrow the fire's head until it dead-centered on the break the hotshot crew was cutting. Then they'd hit any spot fires that cropped up once it got there. No reason to call in the big outfits yet, most of whom were fighting a blaze up north in the Columbia Gorge.

"How'd you do it, Curt?" The three of them flew in a line over the Black, as the burned-over section of a forest fire was called.

"I just fly low and hit the little button that says Tank Release on it when I'm over the flames."

"Ha. Ha. No. How did you get Stacy?"

"'Cause I'm just that good."

"Blind luck," Jasper commented drily as the three of them came up on the fire.

"Truth?" Palo eased in close behind Curt. A glance showed Jasper nowhere to be seen, which meant he was exactly astern. It was becoming the Firebirds' trademark: fly in fast and low in a tight line. Between them, they could lay six hundred gallons—a ton-and-a-half of water—in a tightly-connected clean line or a triple-layered inundation, dead on target. With a nearby water source, they could do it once every two minutes.

"Truth?" Curt left it hanging out there as he dove on the fire and Palo followed him down. They were coming in along the edge of a forested ridge. It was covered in hundred-foot Doug fir and trash alder. If they could keep the flames on the south side of the ridge, the fire would narrow itself as it burned along the sharpening valley which climbed up into the Coast Range.

"Truth is he has no idea," Jasper spoke up. Curt and Jasper went all the way back to grade school, which meant Jasper knew.

Curt sighed his agreement as he released his load over the edge of the fire. "If you really want to know, Palo, you need to ask Stacy. I have no idea what a woman that amazing sees in me."

That wasn't going to happen. If he asked Stacy, she'd want to know why. And if he told her *that*, she'd tell— Wasn't going down that way one bit.

Palo followed Curt's line, then peeled off to tank up. The Siletz River was close by, but it was too narrow with tall trees on both banks for most helos. Their little MD 520Ns could slip right in, lower a fifteen-foot long snorkel to suck up a load, and be on the move twenty seconds later without ever landing. What they didn't have in load-carrying capability—the big Firehawks could carry a thousand gallons to his two hundred— they more than made up in speed and agility.

Speed and agility? How in the world was that supposed to help him with a pixie-tall, Latina-fireball of a woman like Maggie Torres?

# 3

To Maggie, the campfire felt empty that night with just the three women around it.

Amos and Drew had gone into Cave Junction. Two thousand people made it the biggest town for thirty miles in any direction. Two thousand people, four restaurants, and very few bars made the odds of running into them far too likely. Besides, as much as Maggie liked men, that whole scene was getting old really fast.

Over the first couple months of the fire season, she'd already tried out most of the local boys. Very few even made it past the first-drink test.

It was a simple test. Could they share one drink without some remark that was the moral equivalent of the Jimmy Buffet classic, *Why don't we get drunk and screw*.

Even fewer had made it past the second-drink test: would her head hurt more if she finished the second drink, which she never actually did, or if she woke up beside the contender?

And the tourists who hit Cave Junction to visit the Oregon Caves—because no one else in their right minds except a wildland firefighter came out here—were traveling as couples. The Caves weren't really a single guy kind of attraction.

She, Stacy, and Jana didn't even have to change positions with the vagaries of the evening breeze—because there wasn't one. It was so quiet that the smoke rose straight up with only the occasional flicker of sparks. They just sipped their beers and watched the fire and the stars.

At least Amos and Drew—when their brains weren't switching off on them unexpectedly—were good for a laugh, bantering back and forth like twin brothers despite one being black and the other white. Maybe it was a New York City thing.

She was more of an Astoria, Oregon gal. Most of her childhood had been spent at the US Coast Guard Air Station. Sometimes she'd travel with Papa to Cape Disappointment on the Washington State side of the Columbia.

Cape Disappointment: another one of her life's ironies. The major Coast Guard installation in the Pacific Northwest perched close by the mouth of the Columbia River. It had some of the most dangerous waters in the entire country. Some said that there were more wrecks crossing the Columbia Bar than the entire Gulf of Alaska. All three of her sisters had married Coasties, but for her there had only been disappointment. Not a single one of them had been made of the same metal as Papa. Most Coasties wouldn't even give her the time of day once they learned she was Chief Torres' daughter. Her sisters never had that problem, so why did she?

So here they were, three women staring at the warm

coals and flickering sparks. The former Siskiyou Smokejumpers Base had been closed in 1981 after launching over fifteen hundred fire jumps. She could feel the men who had lived here through the years—and not just because of the small museum and historic landmark buildings. It was in the night air. In the smell of dry pine and drier grass.

"Story time," Stacy broke the long silence.

Jana's grunt said she wasn't adverse to the idea, as long as it didn't start with her. She sat far enough back in her folding chair so that only her blonde hair and the steel hooks that had replaced her right hand showed. She could still fly like a demon, but she couldn't fly to fire because she couldn't work the thumb and finger controls on the cyclic. She was their head trainer and ran the business with an iron, or rather a *steel* hand, while her brother flew.

"I know you're both sick of me babbling about being married—"

"Totally," Maggie teased her.

"—so I'll shut up about that for a change. That leaves you, Maggie."

"Oh." That hadn't gone well. She listened to the night and could imagine the ghosts of shouts to "saddle up" over the racket of Pratt & Whitney Twin Wasp radial engines coughing to life on the DC-3 jump planes. It left a silence now broken only by the crackling fire and the occasional flutter of bat wings.

Story time had become something of a tradition among the women of the Firebirds. Ever since the massive misunderstanding that almost had Stacy leaving the outfit, they'd held story time. By telling each other pieces of their past when the guys weren't around maybe they could avoid messing each other up in the future. There weren't many opportunities, but they were slowly getting to know one another better for it.

"When Papa had to work late, I used to ride my bike over to the Astoria, Oregon Airport after dinner. I'd help him service the helos, handing him tools and asking a thousand questions. Afterward we'd sit out like this and watch the stars. Sometimes we'd go across the runways to sit beside the Columbia River and watch the ships come in as the sun set over the Pacific."

"What did you talk about?"

"Not much. Engine mods maybe. Boy trouble, a little. Let's just say that I started looking like this pretty early. Having a *papaíto* who was a USCG mechanic and a chief petty officer helped a lot with that."

"Was he pretty like you?" Jana tried to make it sound as if she might be tempted.

"No. I'm a throwback. The shortest one in the family by eight inches. Just like Nana—my grandmother. Ma's pretty, but not in Nana's league, and all my sisters take after Ma, kinda mostly. Papa is really solid, like a rock. Like Palo I suppose." There was a parallel she'd never thought of. "What is he anyway?"

"A hunk," Stacy was still so newly married that she saw all men as beautiful, wonderful creatures.

Jana snorted and tossed her empty beer bottle toward the small cooler.

At least she and Jana knew it was never that simple.

Maggie waved at the cooler to see if she wanted another, but Jana shook her head in a shimmer of blonde hair.

"You're going to laugh when I tell you what he really is," Jana spoke little louder than the fire. "Palo Akana is

Finnish-Hawaiian. Though I don't remember which of his parents is which."

"Last name Hawaiian, probably his dad," Maggie figured.

"Hunk," Stacy affirmed.

Palo was so quiet that Maggie had never given him much thought. Not awkwardly silent like Jasper—who only crawled out of his shell at all when…Jana wasn't around. Huh! That was interesting.

Palo wasn't Hawaiian large, but neither was he Finnish light. He was dark, handsome, and built rock-solid. He also flew so well that Jana and Curt had hired him, which said a lot about the man. Said a lot about Drew and Amos too—at least their abilities if not their shining personalities.

As if hearing her thoughts, there was the low thrum of a pair of diesel trucks coming along the Redwood Highway. She listened. V8. The deep note of a GMC 6.6 liter under moderate load. Enough tire noise to tell her there was a lot of rubber on the coarse-sealed road: like two pickups with rear dualies and hauling trailers.

"The boys are back."

"What?" Stacy lit up like…a newlywed. The girl couldn't help rubbing it in.

Jana was still twisting back and forth as if seeking the sound, not locating it until they were almost in the parking lot. Probably lost some sensitivity in all those years she'd flown for the US Army's 101st Airborne. Maggie missed those days herself sometimes, but she'd left voluntarily—unlike Jana after an accident took her hand.

With the hard crunch of gravel, the two GMC Denali pickups rolled in, each hauling a gooseneck trailer that had their helos tied onto the decks. They rolled up close to the fire before shutting down and clambering out.

"We killed that sucker!" Curt announced in a loud voice. "This boy needs a beer and a kiss."

"Not in *that* order you don't," Stacy leapt into his arms and Curt looked pretty damn pleased with the change of priorities.

Jasper crossed to the cooler and grabbed a pair of cold ones. He uncapped and tucked one in Curt's hand where it was still wrapped around his wife's back. Then he retreated to the shadows near Maggie—directly *opposite* Jana she noticed. He pulled down his white cowboy hat low enough to hide his eyes, but she'd wager he could still see across the fire just fine. Suspicions ninety percent confirmed.

Did Jana know? Not much got by her, but she wasn't looking toward Jasper either. So maybe not.

Ty, their summertime hired help who'd been off with the guys on the Siletz fire, headed off to get the fuel truck. She really needed to talk to him about relaxing at least *once* in a while. Nah, he was young. He'd learn it on his own. Besides, she was the last person who should teach anyone about relaxing.

Then Palo stepped around the back of the trailers, as if he'd circled to make sure everything had survived the five-hour drive back from the fire site. Or maybe so that she wouldn't notice him. He was like that—all stealth in plain view.

Maggie felt more than the fire's heat flash into her as she noticed where his eyes went. They didn't travel to Curt and Stacy still making a happy spectacle of themselves. They didn't go to Jana as she heckled her brother and sister-in-law. He stood back in the dark, but even by the fading reach of the firelight, she could see that he was looking directly at her.

And it wasn't the way that Amos and Drew did, staring in wonder.

He looked at her like a man fresh saved by a Coastie ocean rescue. The moment he stepped once more onto dry land—as if he'd never thought he'd see it again.

She tried to look away. Wanted to join in on Jana's razzing, though her throat was too dry and she couldn't seem to raise her beer.

Palo didn't flinch aside. She'd bet she could heave an entire rack of crowbars into the ground between his feet and he'd just look down at them, and back up at her.

Having been caught staring, he didn't look away.

And until he looked away, she wasn't going to either.

But he didn't!

How had a girl from Astoria, Oregon ended up in a Mexican standoff with a Finnish-Hawaiian fire pilot?

And what was she going to do about it?

# 4

Palo waited. Waited to come to his senses. Waited for Maggie to blink so that he could convince himself that it wasn't him she was looking at. She never had before except in passing.

Not that he'd done anything to encourage it.

Men like him didn't deserve women like Maggie Torres. It wasn't just her looks. Five-foot-two of curvy Latina with dark brown hair down to her shoulder blades, so thick a man could get lost in it.

She was everything he wasn't.

Smart, funny, and a crazy good mechanic. People lit up the moment she entered a room and sighed sadly when she left them behind. Her easy laugh always brightened any gathering. She always had the quick joke or tease. By the time he thought one up, the conversation had long since moved on.

People barely noticed when he arrived or departed and he was fine with that. He preferred the quiet.

She had quiet moments too, though they were rare. She went silent when she was chasing a mechanical problem, focusing all that skill. But that wasn't it. It was the moment before she'd spotted him, while he was still on the far side of the trailers looking at her through the steelwork of the helos' landing skids.

Quiet. At peace. That's when her true beauty came out and shone brightest for him.

Definitely not the kind of quiet she was at the moment.

She looked across the sparks and darkness like a toreador throwing down the red cape in front of the bull, daring him to make the next move. He could feel the impact of those dark eyes aiming bolts of fire in his direction until he was surprised that the gravel didn't turn to lava all around him.

What would it be like to be with a woman like that? To take her down and hold her close?

Not for him. Not for the kid from the San Francisco streets.

His gang had chosen his first name. "I'm gon' be rich someday! You just see," he'd declared in his five-year old surety. "Rich? You must be from Palo Alto. That's where those rich folk live. We gon' call you Palo." He'd chosen Akana because, when child services grabbed him after he was caught robbing a grocery store at eight, it had sounded cool and Japanese. And Japanese were all smart, rich, and drove BMWs. Instead, he'd been fostered to a guy who drove a rattletrap Ford pickup and flew helicopters for the power company—traveling the high-power lines year in and year out looking for problems. Palo had flown with him whenever he could so that he didn't have to see the string of men his foster mom entertained whenever her husband was gone.

Palo hadn't been along when the helo failed high in the Sierra Nevada. They'd traced it back to the mechanic—a mechanic who lived nowhere close to Maggie Torres' standards. They'd fired the mechanic, hired a new one, bought another bird, and hired Palo to take his foster father's place. He'd flown those same lines for six years before Curt Williams had hired him away.

It had been years before he looked up his own name and decided he was Finnish-Hawaiian to the rest of the world. It was certainly better than whoever he really was and he'd decided to keep the name.

And all he could do was stare across the fire at the most beautiful and amazing woman he'd ever seen and know for a fact that he had no right whatsoever to cross one step closer.

So instead, he nodded to her briefly and turned back into the night.

There he could at least dream that he was more than he was.

5

"What's with you?" Jana called out.

Maggie blinked over at her after Palo faded back into the darkness from which he'd so briefly emerged.

Jana twisted around to look over her shoulder, but there was nothing to see.

Again she asked her question.

"I'm not sure," was the best answer Maggie could find. Why would a man like Palo concede defeat like that? He'd looked beaten before he nodded to her and turned away. "I'm not sure…" But she rose to her feet and had to veer sharply after three steps so that she didn't walk straight into the fire.

"What's with her?" Jana asked no one in particular.

If anyone answered, Maggie didn't hear them.

Palo hadn't gone far. He sat on the tail of the second trailer. It was a low-bed, so he sat with his feet on the dirt, looking up at the stars. This far away the campfire offered only the vaguest silhouette. There was no moon yet and her eyes were only slowly adapting to starlight.

"Hey, Akana," she tried to keep it light.

"Hey, Torres." Palo's tone did remind her of Papa's. It simply said, *yep, here I am.* Hard to read what he was thinking one way or the other.

"Mind if I sit?"

"Help yourself." No shrug, that she could see. No hint of anything, except that she should help herself.

So, she scooted up on the trailer's deck, ending up a little closer to him than she intended, but didn't want to move away either. She knew that not everyone shared her ideas about close personal space. Actually, that was another thing that reminded her of Papa…he was the only one she'd really enjoyed having a closer personal space with. Despite that, she didn't feel any pressure to move away from Palo.

She swung her feet above the dirt for something to do.

"What was that?"

Palo didn't play dumb, which she liked. Instead, she could make out that he was staring at the stars.

So, for a while, she stared with him and watched Orion the hunter and Taurus the bull fighting the battle that they'd been having since the Greeks had named the constellations a kagillion years ago.

"There's a lot to admire about you, Torres," Palo said to the darkness as if it was plain fact.

"It's skin deep, Akana."

"I get that. Not what I was talking about. The way you're put together gets a man's attention, no question about that. It's what's past that I was talking about."

Maggie tried to catch her breath. No one admired her like that since… No. It was time to stop drawing parallels between her Papa and any man she was interested in. It wasn't fair to the man. If she kept comparing Palo to Papa, she'd never see the man as clearly as Stacy saw Curt—loving him with all of his shortcomings. If he—

*Holy Mother!* She had not just thought about being interested in Palo Akana.

But the idea, now that she'd thought of it, didn't sound as crazy as she expected it to.

Palo still sat. It was a comfortable silence, one that wasn't pushing all of her action buttons. It was the kind of silence that invited questions into it.

But she didn't know where to start.

"Finnish-Hawaiian, huh? What was that like?"

Palo was silent so long that she wondered if she'd somehow misunderstood something.

Then he sighed. "Of all the places in the world, you had to start there?"

She didn't know what to say, so she stared at the sky and waited.

# 6

Talking about his past always wrung Palo dry. He wasn't sure the last time he'd been so exhausted. They'd fought fire for four straight days. They'd started this morning at sunrise and only been released at five o'clock. Everyone had agreed they wanted to get back to the Firebirds' base, so they'd driven through the evening and the slow mid-summer sunset to reach the Illinois Valley Airport.

To see the women there, sitting around the fire as if waiting for them, had caught him so off guard. Curt welcomed by Stacy like he was coming home. The crew sitting around the campfire like they all belonged. Palo had never belonged anywhere except for his early days in the gang and flying beside his foster father.

But none of that was what had knocked him back.

Now that he'd spilled his past in the dirt beneath Maggie Torres' feet, it felt as if all life had been ripped out of him. Nothing remained except for the scorched Black.

He'd only told bits and pieces of his past to anyone

before, never the whole thing. It always earned him, "Oh you poor thing," or something like that as if he was a wounded puppy. It hadn't taken him long to learn to keep his mouth shut. Why hadn't he been able to do that around Maggie Torres?

"I went back and looked up missing persons reports. You know, for kids lost around that time," apparently there was even more to dump at Maggie's feet. "You wouldn't believe how many kids every year, just in San Francisco. Almost two thousand: runaway, family abduction, unknowns…"

Still Maggie gave him her silence. He couldn't look down from the sky where his dreams lay to see her reaction. All he could hold onto was that she was still there beside him.

"I figure I belonged to the gang. They were my first memories anyway. A lot of teen pregnancies. Our gang leader would have been thirteen or so back then—could have been my dad, if he even knew. Moral standards and monogamy weren't real priorities when you're trying to survive on the streets. I tried to find them years later, but they'd disappeared into the dust. It was all Pinoy Pride and Nortenos the one time I went looking. Who knows what it is now? Haven't been back."

Maggie rested one of those fine, strong clean hands on his shoulder. They might be covered in grease or fire ash, but they were ever-so clean in other ways.

Here it came. *Poor little boy.* At least she wasn't disgusted and running away, but this wasn't much better. He hated pity.

"How did you become like you are?"

He looked down at her in surprise. The crescent moon had cracked over the Siskiyous while he'd told his tale. It now lit her eyes enough to see that there weren't tears there. Not pity at all. No way she could be impressed, but he didn't know what else to call her look.

"My foster dad. He was a good man. Ex-military pilot. Never spoke about it…or anything else. Real quiet type. Even more than me. Showed me by example what I always figured a man should be. My foster mom didn't set much of an example about women though."

"Where did you learn about them? What a woman *should* be?"

Palo dug down, but couldn't find the words. He'd always thought a woman was what he found in the bars. He'd seen others, women in couples and the like, but they were always at a distance. Somehow *other*.

He flew the lines, endless miles of power looping from one remote tower to the next. Every now and then finding a broken insulator and a dangling line. Other times finding where a tree had fallen and damaged a trestle tower. Illegal, and insanely dangerous, TV antennas rigged high in the steel. Three bodies of sport climbers who hadn't understood the random whimsical nature of the voltages they were messing with.

Coming "to land" only among the male mechanics and other pilots. Women for him spent their lives perched on bar stools. Buying them when he needed one: sometimes with dinner and drinks, sometimes with cold, hard cash.

He'd never thought of women as much else, until he'd seen Maggie Torres lift a wrench and tackle a helicopter like it was an old friend. Stacy and Jana were other examples, now that he thought about it.

But he'd only ever seen Maggie.

7

"Oh," Maggie finally got it. "Me? Palo, you can do better than that."

He just shook his head like a cornered bull.

"I'm like the least girlie girl on the planet. I was such a tomboy that I made Coast Guard jocks feel like sissies. I only put on a dress and flirt in the bars to prove to myself that I'm not a complete lost cause as a woman."

"You're *not* a lost cause," his voice was a low growl. The first emotion he'd revealed in the whole telling of his awful past and it was in the defense of *her* femininity. There was a laugh.

"Palo!" The frustration in her own voice earned her a smile. "No one in their right mind should be attracted to me."

"Everyone in their right mind *is* attracted to you."

"For all of the wrong reasons!" She didn't like that they all wanted her body, not her. But Palo had already listed why he was attracted to her. His reasons were all about her real self and not—well, only a little—about how she looked.

Palo waited her out.

"How come you never said anything? How many times did you sit in a bar and watch me…" Maggie couldn't even finish the sentence. …*flirting with useless men.*

"Don't go to the bars much anymore. Not since I met you."

And he was right. He always had some excuse or other to beg off except when all the Firebirds went as a team.

But Maggie pictured him there anyway. Pictured him sitting quietly at a stool down the end. It was easy to imagine him there—the strong silent type. Easy to imagine his foster dad beside him. She could hear the love, even if he dismissed it. *Two* strong, silent men. Sitting at the end of the bar, sipping their beers. One teaching the other what it meant to be a man just by his steadiness, by his commitment to his work.

And it was far too easy to imagine her not noticing him. Yet in her mind's eye, Palo made all those other boys pale by comparison. She could feel him watching her in her imagination until her entire body tingled for real.

"Palo."

"Uh-huh."

She dropped down on her feet and turned to stand between his knees.

"Palo."

He considered her for a long moment in silence, then his eyes went wide. "No, Torres. You deserve better than me."

"And you don't think that's for me to decide?"

He tried leaning back, but was stopped by the helo anchored to the trailer close behind him.

"Palo."

"Torres, don't!"

"You're not getting off that easy. You've got to at least kiss me once. There is no way that a man can tell me I'm the model of all womanhood and not kiss me to prove his point."

Palo groaned as if in agony.

It was almost enough to make her step back. But she hesitated a moment too long.

He grabbed her and pulled her hard against him until her thighs were pressed against the flat metal edge of the trailer and her upper body was crushed against the wonderfully solid chest of his. Palo had been carved out of granite, fire-hot stone that scorched her fingers to touch as her hands came to rest there.

For all the violence of his embrace, his kiss hesitated half a breath away, then settled upon her lips with all the gentleness of the still night.

*This*, was all she could think. *This* was what she'd been looking for in all those bars and with all those men. Heat, power, tenderness—all fabricated of something that wasn't like any other man but remained fantastically male.

Maggie was so lost in the moment that all she could offer was a small choking cry of shock when Palo pulled back abruptly, forcing her to step away with his hands on her shoulders.

Before she could recover, he was gone into the dark.

The ground weaved beneath her like a storm-tossed rescue boat. Without Palo holding her, it felt as if the lightest breeze—the slightest impetus from a passing owl's wing—would take her to her knees.

"That," Stacy said from where she leaned in the darkness against the helicopter on the other trailer. "Is *exactly* what I've been talking about."

Maggie couldn't even nod.

# 8

He shouldn't have just walked away. But he had to protect Maggie from herself. Palo knew only one use for women—up with the skirt, down with the underwear, and do that deed until they both were done.

That was the lesson he'd seen in the older members of the gang. It was the lesson his foster mom had certainly taught—even offering herself to him when he was man-grown. Instead he'd taken one of the high school cheerleaders for the football team as his first time. Couldn't even remember her first name—might not have ever known her last one.

It was the lesson that every woman in every bar had taught him.

Instead, the moment he'd touched Maggie, his world had shifted. He'd never taken his time kissing a woman. Hell, he'd screwed far more women than he'd ever kissed because that's what women were for.

With Maggie Torres, he'd wanted to give her a gentleness he'd never found—*never imagined*—before.

And she'd responded with an openness and an innocence that had shocked him to the core. Shocked them both apparently. That little cry as he'd stepped her back from the kiss told him more than he'd ever known about her.

Maggie was an innocent. Not a virgin—he wasn't dumb enough to think that, or care. Not unworldly either.

*But* she thought the world shone as a far nicer place than he knew it was.

A part of him had wanted to take her. Tear away her t-shirt to dig his fingers into those perfect, high breasts. Yank down her cute little gym shorts, bend her over, and ram himself home. He knew about that. He knew how to do that.

He knew nothing about how to kiss and hold a woman who sighed her breath into his mouth as he wrapped his arms around her. He'd filled his hands with her rich bounty of hair. Rather than an urge to yank down on it to force her head back—to ravage her neck and chest—he'd wanted to brush it over his face and feel how the soft curls touched lighter than fire smoke.

She had stood, shining in the moonlight, stunned into a small whimper. The violence of his desperate need for her was so close to the surface that she'd known. She must have.

He had wanted her so badly in that instant, that he could no longer trust himself. Another breath filled with her scent, another heartbeat racing because of the feel of her, and he was going to take her down like any bar whore.

Not Maggie.

So he'd slid clear and stalked away into the darkness

not knowing where he was going. He'd finally slept under a tree, having to wait for dawn to figure out where he was and walk the five miles back to the airport.

Thank god he'd arrived just in time for another fire call. It spared him having to face her as they all raced to load up the remaining helos and start the five-hour drive down to Chico, California. A prairie fire was turning its sights on the airport there—with the town not far behind.

## 9

As usual, she, Jana, and Ty drove the three pickup trucks, each towing a pair of MD 520N helicopters on long trailers. In her truck, Maggie had Stacy in the front and Jasper in the back. Curt and Palo rode with Jana and the knuckleheads ended up in Ty's truck.

It always ended up that way and for the first time, she was beginning to understand why. Even if she didn't like it.

She'd tried to maneuver Palo into riding with her and Stacy. Not so that they could talk, exactly. But maybe they'd be able to anyway if he sat up front and Stacy pretended to be asleep in the back.

But that would mean Jasper would have to ride with Jana. He made it clear that wasn't going to happen, by chucking his go-bag in the back seat of her own truck.

Instead it was her and Stacy, with Jasper catching some shut-eye.

"It was one kiss," she'd whispered to Stacy after they

were finally away from Cave Junction. They'd all grabbed breakfast at the River Valley Restaurant. They'd pulled a couple tables together which the waitresses soon buried in tall stacks, waffles, and biscuit-and-gravy combos. Palo had somehow ended up at the opposite end of the long table.

"Uh-uh. Not pulling the wool over this gal's eyes. I *know* what a normal kiss looks like," Stacy sounded entirely too pleased with herself.

Maggie had to remember that she wasn't the dreamy airhead she'd been appearing to be lately. She was a top pilot with an amazing track record against fire. Other than Jana, she was probably the brains of this outfit.

"Is that what happened to him?" Jasper wasn't snoozing off his breakfast the way he'd appeared to be. "He never came back to the bunkhouse last night. Kissed you, huh? Explains what he was talking about."

"What he was talking about?" Maggie wasn't sure she wanted to know.

"Tell us! Tell us!" Stacy twisted around enough to look back, meaning there was no escape now.

"Was asking about how Curt got you, Stacy."

"What did he say?" Stacy went off into her dreamy world voice.

"You think he knows? He told Palo to ask you."

And Stacy sighed happily. "That's my Curt. Just like Jana warned me. The best of men, just not a real deep thinker."

"So how did he get you?" Jasper's tone changed and Maggie wished she could turn to see his expression. His ever-present cowboy hat made him impossible to read in the rearview mirror.

"Blind luck," Stacy sighed.

Jasper harrumphed. "Exactly what he said."

"It's true. He's just this great guy. I haven't had a lot of experience with those but he completely sold me on them. Who's on your horizon, Jasper?" She turned to Maggie when he didn't answer. "We need to find Jasper a girl."

"Not gonna happen," and she could see him pull his cowboy hat down even further, indicating he was done with this conversation. Maggie was sure that she knew the answer he was avoiding.

"Looks like you already found your man," Stacy bubbled happily, missing all of the dynamics.

There was no way that a kiss, one kiss, could mean that. She'd kissed plenty of men, but not one had been like Palo. It was like he was worshipping at the altar, so gentle and sweet that it had wholly taken her breath away. No one had ever kissed her like that before.

She could feel the need in him. Could feel its fire scorching her. Maggie had even felt the violence in him, the need to take so strong, yet held under such perfect control that he could hold her that lightly.

What would it be like to just let herself be taken? To give herself over to a man's desires when what he desired was her? Because he absolutely didn't see her as "just some woman." A man like him didn't need to control himself around "just some woman." He was good-looking, incredibly strong, and there wasn't any doubt in Maggie's mind about his ability to deliver anything a woman could want. She—

"You need a mirror," Stacy broke in on her thoughts as they rolled through Grant's Pass and picked up I-5 south.

"Why?"

"You know that look you keep accusing me of?"

"No!" Maggie definitely had *not* gone all dreamy on a guy after a single kiss.

Though it had been an *amazing* kiss.

## 10

"Not talkin' about that." Palo hunched down in the back seat and wished there was a way he could disappear. He'd already talked more with Maggie last night than he did in most weeks. He was talked out. He was done.

"Well, you did something to her, Palo," Jana was at the wheel, but had twisted the rearview mirror so that she was staring straight at him each time she glanced away from the road.

"I kissed her. That's all I did."

Curt turned to look back at him. "You kissed, Maggie Torres? You lucky shit."

"You're happily married, remember?" Jana reminded her brother.

"Didn't say it was me. Didn't say I was trying to," Curt backpedaled fast. "Just saying that Maggie lets very few men aboard. Damn, brother!" He held up a fist for Palo to do a fist bump with. He sighed and did it because he knew Curt wouldn't let it go until he had.

"Assholes," Jana grumbled as they twisted and

turned down the steep hills before hitting the open flatlands of Medford.

"Hey!" Curt had turned away, but now twisted back to look at him.

"No." It was too easy to guess where Curt's thoughts had gone and he didn't want him telling his sister. He didn't want it getting back to Maggie.

"That's why you were asking how I *caught* Stacy."

"Blind luck," Jana zinged him.

"Why does everyone keep saying that?" Curt faced forward and folded his arms over his chest.

"Think about how amazing Stacy is." Jana kept facing straight ahead, but Palo could feel her smiling.

"Yeah," Curt sighed. "Blind luck. You gotta do better, Palo. Don't let a woman like that slip through your fingers. We're talking about a major keeper."

A couple miles passed in silence, something Curt was never good at.

"Hey! We gotta get you a man, sis."

"Not in this lifetime," she held up the hooks that were her right hand. "Nobody sees me past these."

"Gotta be someone. Come on, Palo. Who do we know that deserves my sister?"

That was the problem.

Did he himself deserve a woman like Maggie Torres?

She *was* a major keeper. But was he?

11

"*Enough* already!" Maggie stood beside his door the moment Palo landed the helo.

She was wearing a wide-brimmed goofy white sun hat with her mechanics coveralls—which she'd hacked off as short shorts. The woman was so damn cute he couldn't stand it.

He was just in from the last run of their fifth day on the Chico fire. It was half an hour to sunset and the little MD 520Ns didn't have the expensive, and heavy, gear to be night-certified. Just as well, they needed eight hours rest out of every twenty-four and that's about all the darkness there was this time of year.

He was hot, sweaty, hungry, and tired.

He was hot for the little slip of a mechanic standing there with her fists propped on the toolbelt hanging slantwise on those ever-so nice hips. Getting sweaty with her sounded even better than a shower. He was hungry for the taste of her. And he was tired of running away.

"I'm a grown woman despite my size."

He wasn't going to argue that point.

"I know what I want."

"Fine," he grunted against a dry throat. Flying over the fire did that. Flying over one in the superheated flatlands of Chico, California could parch a man for life. The two together sucked.

"Fine?" Causing her to blink in surprise.

"Fine." More than fine. "Where and how soon?"

She pointed as imperiously as a queen in a toolbelt, coveralls, and fashionable sunhat could. It was summer and the campus was mostly empty. With the airport smoked out and shut down—though not burned yet—their six helos were lined up in two rows on the open field outside the stadium. The college had opened up one of the dorms for the firefighters.

The rooms were doubles with two small beds and zero sound insulation. He'd bedded enough coeds when he was that age to know. That would never do.

"Get in." When she started to protest, he pulled the door shut in her face.

She huffed around the nose of the helo as he wound the engine back to life. Her hair caught and fluttered in the vagaries of the air turbulence coming off the flattened blades. He pushed in a little bit of negative lift with the cyclic, sucking the air up through the main rotor. It made her hair float up off her shoulders as she clamped a hand atop her hat. Yes, he remembered her hair's lightness in his hands and couldn't wait to touch her again. Why he'd hidden from her for five days was… well, obvious. To be done with that was more relief than a cold shower could ever provide.

Once she'd shed her toolbelt and was buckled in, he took them aloft.

The other helos, which had been coming in behind

him, hesitated when they saw the two of them together through the large windshield. Curt waggled his helo side to side in a cheery wave, as did Stacy. Jasper just flew by. Drew and Amos seemed to stumble in the air.

He was past caring what others thought.

Palo flew them up into the hills east of Chico. The hills climbed quickly in a jumble of eroded valley through the tall buttes. The Big Chico Creek had cut especially deeply and still flowed year-round. Its rollicking course had been turned into a nature park.

"The entrance to Bidwell Park is closed by the fire, they emptied the place out three days ago even though the park itself is safe."

He found the spot he was after and spiraled them down. A giant snag, an old tree long since shed of life and bark, stood tall and weather-whitened over a tiny meadow surrounded by towering fir and spruce. The twenty-seven foot sweep of the MD 520N's rotors was a tight squeeze into the small clearing, but it fit.

Along one edge of the clearing, shaded by a few trees, there was a large pool in the stream formed by a rise of boulders at one end. At the other end, a waterfall splashed loudly into the upper end of the pool.

Maggie had gone quiet and he didn't know what to think. He did the full shut down. Even when he opened the door to let in the cool of the evening, she didn't budge.

He circled around and opened her door.

She unbuckled, stepped down, and into his arms. No kiss, no hug. She simply tucked her hands under her chin and leaned in against his chest. He wrapped his arms around her and wondered if they could stay like this forever.

"Thank you."

"For what? I haven't done anything yet." Maggie rubbed her face on his sweat-stained shirt as if she didn't care that he stank.

"For bringing me here. For letting this be important."

He gathered a handful of that luxurious hair and tugged it just enough to get her to look up at him.

"You *are* important."

She nodded once. Then again. "So are you. I'd have taken you either way. A fun tussle or this. But I wanted to thank you for this."

"That doesn't cut out the fun tussle part, does it?"

Her smile went electric. "Let's find out."

## 12

"Fun tussle," Maggie managed on a half laugh.

Palo managed to grunt an amused agreement that vibrated down her length as she still lay upon his chest.

They lay on one of the helo's emergency blankets spread close beside the stream. They had splashed in wearing their clothes, because they needed washing as badly as their bodies. The clothes had soon been tossed on the bank, but they'd swum back and forth in the fifty-foot pool of Brown's Hole for a long time.

Rather than cooling her off, the delay as they'd floated and talked had given the banked fires time to rekindle and burn anew. Any doubts she had were scorched away when he touched her for the first time as the last ray of sunlight snaked up their canyon to light the pool. His rough hand, softened by the water, had brushed along the side of her breast like an invitation. One she hadn't refused.

Now, hours later, she could only lie atop him and listen to the night in wonder.

The first time, after she'd fished out some of the protection she'd bought this morning, she had let him take and plunder, because the need was so great and burned so hot that it couldn't happen fast enough for her.

The second time, she had taken him. Spending the time to appreciate, to caress, and to feel. *Holy Mother, to feel!* Never had a man made her cry aloud with the pure joy of the moment…her voice had echoed off the basalt walls.

"No way we can keep this from the others. One look at our smiles will give us away." Now, at least, she knew where Stacy's outrageous grin came from.

"Can't keep a damned secret in this outfit anyway." Palo sounded grouchy about it.

"Like you talking to Curt about how he got Stacy?"

Palo groaned.

"So is that what you're looking for? Happy ever after?"

"What about you?" She almost called him on dodging the question, but she didn't know herself and had to think about it.

"Mama and Papa had a great relationship. Even with four girls running around with a thousand demands, they always found ways to be together. They'd hold hands while watching TV. Anything."

"Well? Do you want that?" Palo's voice was so gentle.

She wanted… "More."

"More than happy ever after?"

She hid her face against his chest—she'd never told anyone the last part.

"What?" Palo kissed her on top of the head as he

flipped a blanket over them against the cooling evening. Sensing her silence, he asked again. "What is it, Torres?"

She couldn't ignore a voice like that, so concerned, so willing to listen. But she couldn't do it.

"I just want more. That's all."

She snuggled down once more on his glorious chest, hiding and she knew it. She tucked her head under his chin. His breathing slowed, then his hands slipped off her back until he lay limp beneath her.

This?

She listened to him sleep in the darkness.

*This* she most *definitely* wanted. For as long as she could have it.

13

"What the hell, Palo?" Curt was right in his face and he couldn't do anything about it because Curt was absolutely right.

He'd screwed up…in flight! The Firebirds had labored long and hard to perfect tight formation flying in the chaotic air currents over a forest fire. Which meant that when he screwed up today, he'd nearly taken three other birds down with him. It was only by some piloting miracle, and a lucky updraft that any of them were still alive.

"Well?"

He could only shrug. He had no idea what had happened.

"You uncaring son of a bitch! You're grounded!" Curt stalked off.

The other pilots who'd gathered to listen—though Amos had still been so shaky that he'd sat on the ground —looked at him in silence a moment longer.

He shrugged again. It wasn't that he didn't care. It was that he didn't know what had happened. He'd never come so close to dying. And to take others out with him *was* unforgivable.

Grounded.

Exactly what he deserved. But what the hell was he supposed to do now?

A hand rested on his back. After a month of living with and making love to Maggie Torres, he knew that touch better than his own.

He couldn't turn to face her.

"I saw the video." All of the Firebirds had multiple cameras to record their successes. Now they had recorded his failure. "What happened?"

Since shrugging hadn't worked, Palo tried shaking his head.

"Don't you *dare* brush me off, Palo Akana!" He'd only roused Maggie's temper a few times over the last month, but she'd given him a deep and abiding respect for it.

"I'm not. I really don't know what happened."

With her lightning quick change, the woman who came around in front of him was all sympathy and worry, not anger.

"One moment we were flying clean. Then I lost a chunk of time. Seconds at most. But it was just a blank." Each word hurt to bring up, but to answer the fear in Maggie's eyes he forced himself to find them.

"Eleven seconds," she whispered. "You flew at a hundred and seventy miles an hour for eleven full seconds without a single course change—not even a wiggle in flight. Like you'd been hypnotized by that tree."

He remembered *that* tree. An old monster of the forest reached up almost three hundred feet. Every inch of it a roaring torch and he'd flown at it like a moth seeking the flame. He'd come to—eleven full seconds? Unthinkable!—less than a second from the tree. He'd slammed the cyclic sideways, cutting a hard turn, almost putting his rotor blades through Stacy's helo. She'd hauled back, letting him pass mere feet below her, but her action had Jasper and Drew nearly ramming her from behind. His own correction had been so hard that only a lucky updraft had kept him clear of the burning treetops—though it had almost cooked him alive.

That's when the shakes hit him.

Maggie wrapped her arms around him and held on. He didn't deserve it, but she did.

Grounded? He should be cashiered and have his license revoked.

"I really screwed up, Maggie." He leaned down far enough to bury his face in her hair. "I don't know why. I just don't…"

"Shh!" She stroked her hands down his back. "We'll figure it out. I believe in you. We'll solve this."

And that's when he remembered.

He knew exactly what had gone wrong up there. It wasn't *that tree* that had hypnotized him.

The truth was even worse than he'd feared.

Palo tried to push Maggie away. When it didn't work, he tried harder. When she finally let go, he was pushing her hard enough that she tumbled over backward, landing hard on her butt.

"Steer clear of me, Torres. Oh shit! Please just stay away."

His Pontiac Firebird was parked by the small hut he'd shared with Maggie whenever they'd been in camp over the last month, as if he deserved to have a place to call his own.

Keys in his pocket.

He climbed in and was headed out of the parking lot before Maggie was even back on her feet. He punched up through the gears until the Redwood Highway was a blur. Fifty twisting miles to the coast at Crescent City, California. Maybe he wouldn't stop. Just do everyone a favor and plow straight into the ocean and put himself out of everyone's misery.

Palo knew he wouldn't. He'd never once thought of suicide, not even listening to his foster mother grunt away for the third trick of the night on the other side of the thin bedroom wall. But there was a part of himself he'd kill if he could.

And it wasn't the part that had fallen in love with Maggie Torres.

14

"Keys! Now!"

Curt pulled them slowly out of his pocket with a puzzled expression on his face. Maggie grabbed them out of his hand and raced over to his classic Trans Am.

"Hey!" Curt shouted after her, but she ignored him. All she knew was that the man she loved had just driven away from her without explanation and that her Denali pickup wasn't up to catching Palo's Firebird.

She slammed out of the parking lot spraying a great fan of gravel. She was in second by the time she hit the road and the tires chirped hard on the pavement when they caught.

Hammering through the tiny hamlet of O'Brien, she spotted Carl on the road in his police cruiser. The speed limit for town was down to fifty, just as she was cracking ninety in fourth gear. He chirped his siren at her as she flew by, but the Firebirds all had black cars with red flames on them—except of course Curt's which had the red and gold Firebird on the hood. They were known and he let her go by. She saw his smile flash when they were just even and he chirped the siren again in greeting. Maggie would have to be extra nice to him next time.

After she caught and killed that Finnish-Hawaiian bastard street punk from San Francisco, Palo Akana.

She spotted his car just after the long straightaways of Oregon ended and they flashed across the California border. The narrow two-land road grew narrower and began twisting down a sharp canyon between densely forested hills. She kept her foot in it and would have to remember to tell Curt that his right front suspension needed to be tightened up and his carb was running a little lean—because damn this was a sweet ride and it should be treated right.

California CHIPS were notoriously less tolerant than Oregon's Staties. Thankfully, Palo wasn't pushing it, so she caught up fast.

She took him on a blind corner, then slammed on her brakes as she cut in front of him. He skidded into a four-wheel drift, leaving long black streaks on the pavement before he bounced into a dirt pullout high on a curve. Lucky for him she hadn't caught him on the other side of the curve or he'd be nose down in Griffin Creek right about now which sounded fine to her.

She thought about ramming him, but didn't want to ding the boss' pretty car. If she'd been in her Denali she have run right over the top of Palo's old Firebird.

"Who the hell taught you to drive, woman?"

"*Mi papa*, so don't go there!" She'd never been so mad in her life as she stormed up to him.

He leaned back against his car with folded arms over his chest and glowered down at her.

"And don't be trying that shit either, Akana. You do *not* walk away from me. You can yell at me, cry on me, make love to me, but you do *not* walk away. Ever!"

Palo watched her for a long moment. Then he reached out a hand and it was all she could do to not flinch away as he brushed her cheek. "Never seen you cry, Maggie."

"I don't." *Ever!* But his finger was wet. She brushed at her cheeks and felt the hot water there. "I don't!" Insisting sounded stupid, but it was all she had.

"Okay," Palo shrugged and refolded his arms.

No point in hitting him, her fist would just bounce off. "Where's a crowbar when I need one?"

He crossed to his trunk, opened it and pulled out a car jack handle. He handed it to her.

"Do your worst." And he looked even sadder than she felt.

"You just don't walk away," she threw the jack handle into the dirt where it stuck point first and quivered. "Mama did that. I can't have that twice in my life."

He blinked, just once. Palo might not talk much, but he wasn't slow. "But you said…"

"After we were all grown and gone. One day she just —left. Her note to Papa said, 'Don't come looking for me.' That's all. Took her car, her clothes, and one half of the bank account. Nothing else. I mean nothing. Not photo albums, not a can of god forsaken soup. We never heard from her again. Just about killed Papa."

"Aw, shit, Torres. Okay, never walk away from you. Got it."

Struggling for air, refusing to give in to the sobs that wanted to follow the tears, she forced herself to look once more at Palo. Unable to speak, she could only wait.

"So why did I, huh?" He grunted to himself.

Maggie could only nod in response.

He looked up at the sky so long, that she too looked aloft. Low alder and high Douglas fir. The two-lane road was deep in the valley cut by Griffin Creek. She could hear it bubbling away in the background. Above was a slice of blue. It was an Oregon blue, pure except for a dusting of sea mist, softening without stealing the beauty of the color.

"The only place my life has ever made sense was up in that sky. Flying with my foster dad. Working the lines after he went down. Flying to fire with Curt. I don't know how to be down here on the ground."

Again he reached out to brush a finger along the line still warm from her tears, but this time it was a caress.

"I love you, Maggie. That's what happened to me up there. It wasn't the damned tree. I figured out that I love you. Nothing in my life prepared me for the power of that realization. You share your bed with me, which is a gift I never imagined. But how can a lost cause like me ever give you what you want? What you deserve? Family? Children? Happy ever after? I can hear it in your voice. I can see it in the way you breathe. I can't give you that."

"Why not?" Maggie barely breathed the words. Had her mother ever loved her father as much as she loved this man? Impossible, or she'd never have left. She'd married a Coastie who loved his job as much as his family and been unable to live with that choice.

Palo just flapped his hands at himself, then let them fall by his side.

"I…" why were these things so hard to say? Maggie tried again. "I love you, too. I love Palo Akana."

He squinted at her. Because, like the good man he was, he'd never looked away.

"Yes, he pulled a crappy set of cards, but look at who he's become. And don't give me any *mierda* about genetic heritage. Whether they were teens in a gang or a drug-blasted whore, look at who you made, Palo. Palo is—*you are* an incredible man. And if you don't believe me, ask any one of the Firebirds."

"Don't think any of them are real happy with me at the moment."

"Feh!" Maggie waved that aside. "That's only because you almost killed them today. They'll get over it."

As if in answer, Drew and Amos rolled up in their black-and-flame GTOs. Stacy, Curt, Jana, Jasper, and Ty piled out as well.

"What are you all doing here?" Maggie knew from a month's experience that she needed peace and quiet to deal with Palo. She didn't need this!

"The way you tore outta there, Torres," Curt stuck his thumbs in his pockets and rocked back on his heels. "I figured Palo might need some backup."

"And them?" Maggie waved a hand at the others.

"We're talking Maggie Torres here. You don't think I'm dumb enough to take you on by myself." The others were grinning at her. Wasn't a man or woman in the outfit that didn't top her by at least six inches.

She considered reaching down and grabbing Palo's jack handle out of the dirt.

To hell with them all. She turned back to Palo.

"Well, looks like we get to do this in front of everyone." Maggie knew she was right and not even the collected Firebirds were going to stop her. "Are you spending the rest of your life with me? Or are you chickenshitting out because you had a crappy past? In which case, you can just keep right on driving."

Palo looked at her a long time, then glanced at all the cars pulled up around his. "Looks like I'm all parked in."

"Not good enough, Palo."

He grunted. "That's the challenge. Who's good enough for Maggie Torres?"

"C'mon, Palo." "Do it, Akana." The others were soon making so much noise that she knew there was no way for him to hear what she said, but she said it anyway, as one final plea.

"You are."

After a long pause—just looking her directly in the eyes—he nodded. Exactly like that time before he disappeared into the darkness around the campfire.

Maggie could feel her heart breaking.

But this time, he looked back up at her.

"You sure?" he mouthed silently.

Now it was her turn to nod—just like the *repeat after me* of a wedding.

He took a deep breath, then moved a single step forward and went down in front of her on one knee.

If the rabble of the Firebirds had been loud before, they exploded and Maggie could barely hear herself think.

So, when Palo reached out his hand, she took it and knelt before him.

"Together," she told him as the applause took over from the cheers.

Being a man of few words, he just pulled her into the safest place in the world and held her tight against his beautiful chest, just as she knew he would for all their days.

# WHEN THEY JUST KNOW

***Jasper Jones*** *flew as Curt's wingman since he moved in next door at the age of six. But Curt's stunning older sister? He never could talk to her when they were kids. Time hasn't fixed the problem.*

***Jana Williams*** *holds herself together by the thinnest of threads. She lost her dream job as an Army helo pilot the day she lost her hand. And with that, her sense of self worth.*

*But nothing prepared her for the impact the right man could have on her life and her heart.*

## INTRODUCTION

I had finally cornered Jana. I'd married off her brother, found a happy-ever-after story for her best friend, and she was fast running out of excuses as to why she wasn't next up at bat.

A woman who is convinced she's no longer feminine. So many women I've met feel this way. Perhaps due to image issues or abuse or... Well, a topic for some other time. But one woman particularly stuck in my mind as I was considering Jana.

Now the two have nothing in common...except for how they viewed themselves and they were both blonde (though I didn't recall the latter until writing this sentence).

I met her in a remote corner of the Australian Outback. I was riding my bicycle around the world after burning out of corporate America. She was seeing a little of Australia after leaving her Australian boyfriend, who she'd followed from her native Finland. We spent several days in small kayaks exploring the canyons of Katherine Gorge in Nitmiluk National Park in a mixed group including a couple of Germans and an Israeli. She was barely half my age and one of the gentlest and most beautiful women I'd ever met.

We talked of our home countries and many other things; she was very smart and fascinated by everything. It was only as we paddled the last few hundred yards of the journey that she told me about why she was there.

Her ex-boyfriend had completely controlled her by always finding ways to convince her that she was neither smart nor pretty. He'd kept her trapped by convincing her that nobody else would ever want her or be even the little bit kind that he was—or claimed he was. She finally recognized that and left him, but some part of her still believed he was right.

There are these moments that sometimes slip by. Moments when 20-20 hindsight tells us what we should have said, should have done. And there are some of those missed opportunities that I still regret to this day.

This was not one of those. This time I said it when it counted, standing side by side on an unlikely boat dock in the middle of the Australian Outback. I told her what I really thought of her and how sorry I was for the years of age and differing destinations that separated us. I told her just how smart and beautiful I thought she was and asked her to remember that. At her shell-shocked whisper, "Really?" I could only nod.

It took me weeks more of riding to begin to understand her disbelief. I can still feel the heat of her tears on my shoulder when she hugged me; the first and last time we touched in our three days together. No address, no idea what happened to her after the moment I rode my bicycle away. But it is one of those times that I feel I was in the right place at the right time for someone.

I wanted that for Jana, except I wanted it to be ever-after for her as I hope it was for that lovely girl I crossed paths with a quarter of a century ago.

# 1

*J*ana Williams sat on a lawn chair beside the Denali pickup, clicking her hooks together while staring at the smoke-gray sky. She should be doing paperwork, checking bank balances (always a serious worry, though not as bad as at the start of their first-ever firefighting season), following the feeds from the six MD 520N firefighting helicopters that made up the Firebirds team…something constructive.

Instead, she was parked in the summer- and wind-parched landscape of Oregon's Columbia River Gorge beneath a smoke-stained, dark Purgatory of a sky, while wildfire threatened the farms around Hood River. The tarmac of Ken Jernstedt Airfield shimmered with the summer heat, hazing the tied-down small airplanes almost to invisibility though they were only a few hundred meters away.

And the most useful thing she could think to do was clicking her hooks.

It had started as an innocuous habit.

Back before she'd lost her right hand, she'd had a

habit of fooling with her hair when she was worrying at a problem. She'd found a much-needed distraction in the tactile slickness as it ran through her fingers, so smooth and fine that it almost didn't feel as if it was there at all. It was like playing with golden water. She'd wind it around her fingers one way, then the other. And while some portion of her mind and body had been distracted doing that, she'd been able to think.

Thinking seemed to come much harder now.

After the accident and the end of her Army career, she still had the habit. But her hair snagged painfully in the mechanism of the hooks. Left-handed hair fiddling hadn't been nearly as satisfying. Besides, that hand was now twice as busy as ever because it had to do most of the work of both hands. If she was going to lose a hand, why couldn't it have been the left one? It still took her forever to sign a distorted version of her name, and fancy stuff like tying shoelaces, just totally sucked.

It was even worse when, like now, she was worrying at a problem but didn't even know what it was.

Now she really needed some right-handed distraction, as if her phantom hand was still sending encrypted orders after the dropped Hellfire missile had crushed it past recovery. She supposed that she should feel lucky that the missile hadn't exploded when the arms tech had misfastened the mount on her Sikorsky MH-60 Blackhawk. Jana had wiggled it during a preflight check of her aircraft—and it had let go.

Had her hand made the difference in easing the impact of the hundred-pound missile hitting the steel deck of the aircraft carrier? Had she averted disaster or just pointlessly sacrificed her hand? No one could say for sure. The stupid medal they gave her as a replacement for her hand certainly didn't answer the question.

On her more cynical days—she tried not to think of them as morose or, god forbid, depressed—she'd wonder if she'd have been better off letting the damn thing fall and explode. Instead, she was left to appease her phantom hand and wonder.

Clicking her hooks together had taken some practice. She had to extend her arm to increase the distance between the hooks and where the harness anchored in a strap that ran behind her back and around to her left shoulder. She could also hunch her left shoulder forward. Either technique would stretch the distance and open the hooks; shrink it and the rubber band at the hooks' base pulled them back together. Her innocent finger-twirl had turned into a shoulder twitch.

Jana often debated whether it would be more or less satisfying if her hooks didn't have rubber gripper pads on the insides. It was more of a soft tap than a satisfying metallic click. Maybe…

Maybe she was totally coming apart. No real question about that actually.

"Nice to just stop for a minute," Maggie Torres, the Firebirds miracle helicopter mechanic, plummeted into the chair beside her. She handed over a bottle of water still slick with condensation before opening her own.

Jana appreciated that Maggie never tried to second guess or help. They'd had a discussion of what Jana could and couldn't do with her hooks, and Maggie had never forgotten once. Whether it was Maggie-the-mechanic or Maggie-the-friend who remembered, Jana didn't ask. Friends had always been a tricky thing for her and she didn't like to question what few tenuous ties she had to the world of fully configured humans.

Jana stretched her right elbow out and down and could feel the tension on her left shoulder as the harness took up the slack. She spread the hooks over the bottle's plastic top, then eased the tension. The hooks clamped down hard. With a sharp twist of her left hand, she got it unscrewed.

The chill water felt good sliding down her raw throat. The summer's late afternoon heat, the smoky air, and feeling like shit had left her throat achingly dry.

"How's the crew?"

Jana shrugged, one shoulder, because two would open her hooks and she'd have to fish the bottle cap out of the scrub grass. Instead, she waved her hooks at the radio she'd propped up on the pickup's bumper. That motion made her drop the cap anyway. She ignored it. Just as she'd been ignoring the radio.

They both listened for a moment.

"Sounds like normal flight operations to me," Maggie surmised.

Jana had to agree. Today's mission for the Firebirds was saving farms: house, barn, and livestock—any orchards were an optional bonus. After half a season together, it was easy to pick out the team's voices. Though one of them always sounded strange to her ears.

Jasper Abrams, her brother's best friend, never spoke in camp, only in the air. Occasionally he would grunt at her brother—who led the Firebirds even if his wife Stacy was a better pilot. But that was about all Jasper ever did on the ground and even that was rare.

Whereas in the air—

2

"Hey! You *can* hit the side of a barn." Jasper slid in close, flying his helo in the Number Two slot behind Curt's.

He was also close enough to see the results of the unexpected downdraft over the barn. The faded red barn was an old-style high-peaked roof with a hayloft above and cattle below. The fire-driven wind scooted fast over the top of the tall structure and created a Venturi effect turbulence wake on the backside of the barn. Curt's load of water had been dumped, and then been sucked into the low pressure zone. Rather than dousing the encroaching fire, it had washed fifty years of grime off the side of the barn.

"Of course you can't hit the fire to save your life." Now that Curt's drop had revealed the effect, Jasper was able to anticipate and use it. He dumped his two hundred gallons a second later than instinct said to. As he flew away, he twisted the helo sideways so that he could see the results. The fifteen-hundred pounds of water was sucked in by the backdraft and slammed into the fire with a perfect drop.

Amos whooped out a cheer as he blasted the rest of the fire into the ground. One more pass by the three of them to make sure the fire traveled around the barn and not through it—then they could move on to the neighbor's. After that there was a long bend in the Columbia River that would serve as a firebreak for the fire to die against.

The late afternoon light was lost in long loops of the smoky sky. This fire wasn't big enough to call the heavy teams off the burn out near Spokane, Washington. It was Firebirds sized.

"Show us the way, oh fearless leader," Jasper twisted back into line behind Curt. He wasn't sure why he was in such a good mood. It wasn't often that Curt messed up even a little, and he liked getting a dig in on him. They'd been toe-and-heel since elementary school. Their rivalry had always been evenly matched—in the air and on the ground.

Until now.

Curt had found the woman of his dreams. Stacy Richardson certainly flew and looked like one. He wasn't envious—Stacy wasn't really his type even if she was Curt's. It was part of what had always worked between them. There'd only been a couple times that they'd ever gunned for the same girl…but Jasper's heart had never really been in it when they did overlap.

The golden hills of Washington leaned down over the Columbia as they flew over to retank their helicopters. The light brown of dry summer grasses and the green swatches of conifers so dark that they looked black against the grass. The river itself flowed slow and wide.

To the south the towering peak of Mount Hood was mostly obscured, the glaring white glaciers only peeking through at opportune moments like a white firebrand in the sky.

For Jasper there'd always been one girl who overshadowed them all.

But fourteen-year-olds didn't get to go out with their best friend's eighteen-year-old sister. By the time he was finally out of high school, she was leaving college and headed straight into the Army. His and Curt's graduation had been the same day as Jana's, so there hadn't even been a road trip from Portland, Oregon down to UC Berkeley. She'd gone straight from graduation to Fort Rucker, Alabama as an Aviation Officer.

The woman who'd come home on leave had been almost unrecognizable and had left him beyond his normal tongue-tied. Her long blonde hair chopped jawline short and her cross-country runner body turned powerful and sculpted. She'd also had an equally chiseled aviator boyfriend in tow that had almost killed him to see.

And if Jasper didn't pay attention, he was going to fly straight into Curt's rotors and kill them both for real.

He slid thirty meters to the side and descended to a low hover over the Columbia River. The water here flowed deep and smooth, reflecting their helicopters off its glassy dark blue.

He dropped the snorkel hose into the water and kicked on the pumps. He kept one eye on the gauge as he sucked up two hundred gallons into the helo's belly tank in twenty seconds. He kept the other eye on the lazily flowing river, slowly adding lift to maintain his altitude as he added sixteen-hundred pounds to a helicopter that weighed only that much when empty.

Amos settled beyond him so that they hovered in a long line over the river.

Curt was up and away well before Jasper due to his momentary fumble.

Did Jana have to be so damned distracting?

She'd come back from the Army a broken woman. He knew the loss of her hand ate at her. But losing her career and the Dear Jana from her fiancé—which made him both thrilled and have a serious desire to bust the guy's balls for deserting her—had really thrown her for a loop.

For lack of anywhere else to be, she'd taken to staying at Curt's while they flew firefighting for Columbia helicopters. She'd started to look like she was going to rot in place as she went quietly stir crazy.

He'd joined and eventually captained the high school cross-country running team just as Jana had four years ahead of him. And when he remembered that, he'd shown up at Curt's apartment one day and tossed her running shoes at her.

"Let's go," were the first words he'd said directly to her since his highly lucid, "Oh, man!" when she came home with one less hand than she'd left with.

She'd glared at him from the couch. One-handed or not, she was still the most amazing woman he'd ever seen. She'd finally barked out a sharp, "Fine!" and put on the shoes. Her balance was an issue for the first mile or so. After that, they just ran. Every day before he left for work. She even started coming out to the fireline.

They never spoke, but they ran together almost every morning for the last three years. It was a strange relationship, but it was the best one he'd ever had.

Then when her and Curt's parents had died, it had taken everything just to survive that. They'd been second parents to him, but his best friend and Jana had barely made it through. But they had, and now they flew.

He, Curt, and Amos doused the last of the fire at the barn and were soon chasing the flames as they started on the neighbor's apple orchard. Here, each tree saved was precious. No swatch of annual wheat, but living tree with plenty of years to bear fruit.

Amos and Curt were still ragging each other about something.

But all Jasper could think was how Jana had looked during this morning's run. Her hair was again long, just over her shoulders—the color of sunshine. She ran in gym shorts and a tight t-shirt. Rather than a fire shirt, honoring whatever wildfire they'd recently flown to, it was a helicopter shirt—*Helicopters don't fly, they beat the air into submission.* That described Jana perfectly.

She knocked the breath out of him every single time he looked at her.

A fact he'd never told anyone. Especially not his best friend.

"Let's bring it home, buddy."

"Yep!" Jasper did his best to join in. "We beat that one into submission." And they had. The fire hadn't gotten anywhere near the last barn. They'd even saved a significant portion of his fruit orchard.

"Got a hot lady waiting for me." Curt always had to rub it in.

"Asshole!" Twelve of the last thirteen hours had been in the air. The idea that he was going back to his woman had Curt supercharged despite the hard day. Jasper was going to creak when he climbed down.

"Stacy's got you so whipped, my friend." Curt's wife had him completely wrapped around her pinkie.

"Absolutely!" Curt took full ownership of the slur.

What was Jasper supposed to do with someone that ridiculously pleased with his life?

"I got Stacy. Palo got Maggie. My new mission is getting you a hot babe."

"Me, too," Amos called over the radio.

"What?" Jasper could deal with Amos. "We all thought you and Drew were like forever-after-together dudes." The two of them joked and bickered like twins, even during babe-reconnaissance at the local pub.

Amos could only sputter in protest.

Jasper didn't need some hot babe. He had a woman waiting…

Except she didn't know it and it was becoming clear that he was never going to tell her. Because as long as he never asked, the answer would never be "Hell no!" He didn't think his ego could take that. And he'd rather be part of Jana's life and never have her, than not be around her at all.

# 3

Jana waited as the first three helos returned from the firefight to land on the tarmac at Jernstedt field. Stacy landed first, with Palo and Drew hot on her heels, because none of the pilots could keep up with Stacy. At each helo, Jana would plug in her tablet computer and download all of the flight data and video. The Firebirds were partially financed by the insurance companies for all of the structures they saved and this documentation was their income in a very real way.

She ignored the pain of even touching a helicopter each time, trying to accept that she couldn't fly it. Why couldn't she have lost a foot? Feet were simple. All they had to do was push on a rudder pedal. But without a hand, the complexities of the multiple controls on the head of the cyclic joystick were beyond her capacity.

The ache in her heart was good though. It reminded her that she was alive. Like the ache in her body when she ran each day with Jasper.

He'd saved her life with that running. She hadn't

been in complete despair yet, but she'd been able to feel the end lurking off in the distance. Unable to do the only thing she'd ever loved—to fly—what was left for her? And Jasper had reminded her of something she'd forgotten: the simple joy of running.

For a long time that daily run was her lifeline. It was almost an illness when they missed a day. She never ran alone. Even though he never spoke to her, it had felt disloyal to run without him. It was stupid, she knew, but it was Jasper who had reconnected her to…herself.

Whoever the hell that was.

Maggie rushed up to Palo's helo the moment the engine cycled down and practically threw herself into the cockpit.

Stacy looked up at the sky as she stretched out the kinks of a long day aloft.

"He's five minutes out," Jana told her as she plugged her tablet into Stacy's helo.

Her new sister-in-law flashed a smile at her. "Am I that obvious?"

"Yes."

Stacy laughed. "I'm just so happy. I keep waiting to wake up."

"Don't," Jana actually gave Stacy a one-armed hug that surprised them both. She stepped aside quickly.

"I can't thank you enough times for hiring me."

"Or for letting you have my little brother. I know, you keep telling me," which came out kinda crappy—which was more about her pain-in-the-neck little brother than Stacy. "You're welcome to him," which didn't sound much better.

Stacy was eyeing her like she was a grenade that might or might not still have a pin in it.

"Seriously, Stacy. I've never seen Curt happier than when he's with you. Let's call it sisterly jealousy and leave it at that."

"Okay, Jana." It was a stiff response by Stacy standards who had every bit of naturally bubbly that Jana had never been able to cultivate.

"Shit! I'm being a crappy sister-in-law." She unplugged her tablet from the helo and prepared to move on.

"Jana," Stacy stopped her with a hand on her good arm. Stacy looked right at her with those big brown eyes of hers that had sucked her brother right in. "You're my idol—you know that, right? *You* are the woman I keep trying to be."

Jana's jaw didn't go loose, but it felt as if it should. She had no idea what to say to that except perhaps recommend her sister-in-law get some serious counseling.

"You're so strong. I know my husband's shortcomings. I guess they're part of what I love about him. I know that *you* are the one who built the Firebirds. I'd never have thought to do something like that."

"I didn't think it up, he did."

"Really? Curt? That doesn't sound like him at all."

And she was right. Curt was a straight-ahead guy's guy. A good and patient leader, but not one for thinking outside of the box. He was in charge because he was the kind of guy that people flocked to and stuck with. She'd only ever achieved that by being a better pilot than everyone around her. When Curt had met Stacy, a pilot better than he was, he hadn't competed with her—he'd married her.

The second half of the Firebirds entered the

airfield's pattern and swooped down the runway before carving a final turn into the section of the airfield allocated for their use. Even though the fire was beaten, the upper atmosphere was still thick with dust and smoke. They were definitely getting "red at night." It wasn't even sunset and the sky was bloody.

She and Stacy stood together and watched them land and shut down. No need to glance at the tail number to see who flew which of the otherwise identical birds.

Amos rushed to be first on the ground. The instant he was down, he and his best pal Drew would be off to the motel to clean up. The rest of the crew would catch up with them at the pub where they'd be chatting up women with easy success.

Curt did his usual straightforward: fly here, land there.

Jasper flew the way he ran—dead smooth, stretching out those long legs of his to eat up the distance. Everything about him integrated into a single motion.

Smooth even as he climbed out of the cockpit and pulled on his ridiculous trademark cowboy hat—as if a man who stood six-foot-three had a height inferiority complex.

"You know that your family left Texas when you were four."

"Six." It had become their standard greeting—never anything more. This time was no exception.

His family had moved in next door. Six-year-old Curt had been instantly enamored of Jasper's cool hat. He'd been at that cowboys-are-cool age.

At ten, Jana had been too self-conscious and sophisticated a girl to deign to notice him beyond trying to be nice to their new neighbor—mostly because it got her little brother out of her hair.

Jasper had lived in the thing then just as he did now. He wore it every day, even when they went running. No amount of razzing in school had deterred him. Jana had learned a lot from watching a much younger Jasper stand by the firm conviction of his beliefs. He'd made her wonder what *she* believed in.

And now? Without the Army, without her hand, the only thing she believed in was the Firebirds. It was enough to keep her sane, marginally. *One day at a time, Jana.* Her mantra ever since she'd woken up without her hand.

Jasper continued to loom above her.

Curt and Stacy were busy doing their newlywed greeting thing.

She wished they'd wait until they were back in their room—or another state. It was petty of her, but all their antics did was make her that much more uncomfortable two steps from the silent Jasper.

"I'll just get your data," she stepped around Jasper who wasn't moving.

He nodded his hat, his dark eyes almost invisible beneath the brim.

She'd only made it two more steps past him when Stacy called out.

"Hey, Jana. Curt says that the Firebirds was actually Jasper's idea."

Curt nodded as Jana's gaze swept over him on her way to face Jasper.

Jasper remained frozen in place with his back to her for several seconds. Then he turned slowly to face her.

"But he never said a word. Not in all that planning."

She'd given up addressing him directly as he never spoke to her—directly *or* indirectly.

"No," Curt stepped over. "He had it all hashed out when he ran it by me over beers one night. You know, I've been meaning to ask you since forever, Jasper, what the hell do you have against my sister?"

Jasper didn't turn to Curt, but continued to look right at her.

She wanted to fool with her hair, or click her hooks, or something, but instead remained in a frozen stillness waiting for the answer. It didn't feel like hate, but he certainly never spoke to her.

"It goes back since I can remember," Curt never did know when to keep his mouth shut. "Did she piss on your cowboy hat the day you moved in or something?"

"Nope," Jasper answered Curt without looking away from her.

"Then what? I mean—" Curt jolted like he'd been pinched. "What?" he turned on Stacy. So Stacy had pinched him.

*Go, girl!*

She just rolled her eyes at him. "Come along, dear." And she towed a bewildered Curt away, leaving her alone with Jasper.

Something in his look kept Jana's voice stuck in her throat.

The fuel truck's diesel engine thudded by them as the tanker moved in to refuel the helos. The on-board pump ground to life as the service tech started down the line pumping out Jet A gas. The sharp bite of kerosene accented the wood smoke still hovering in the air.

"I thought up the Firebirds for you after your parents died," Jasper finally spoke to her. It felt as if it was the first time in years. His voice was low and soft. Impossible to disbelieve. Impossible to ignore. The loss of her parents had been a gut shot to them all. It had sent her spiraling down all over again.

"For me?" She managed.

He nodded his head, which was much more about his hat.

"Like the running after the Army," which had gotten her out of the darkest place she'd ever been.

Again the nod.

"Your idea was that poor Jana needed therapy, so you provided it?" Her voice was rising now.

Enough that the fuel truck driver was looking her direction.

"No. I—"

"Poor crippled Jana needs some asshole to take care of her because she can't take care of herself anymore!" Rather than going louder, she felt her voice go low and nasty…and she couldn't stop it. "Well, I don't need anybody. And I sure don't need you, Jasper Jones."

He remained unmoving throughout her tirade.

The words were out there and she could never take them back.

To hell with the last three helos' data.

To hell with the money that data represented.

To hell with her brother and his ever-so-happy life.

"To hell with you, Jasper Jones."

If she hadn't cried when she lost her hand, she sure as hell wasn't going to cry now.

Instead she turned away.

Helo in front of her.

Get in! Fly away! Now!

She placed a foot on the small steel pad on one of

the skid's legs. Got her other foot up and into the cockpit.

That's when six years of habit flying the Black Hawks betrayed her.

She reached out with her right hand to grab the handhold and pull her upper body in.

Except she no longer had a right hand.

# 4

Jasper watched her go. The words he'd feared since the day he'd first spotted the sun-blonde girl next door had finally happened. The only door he really cared about other than Curt's friendship had just been slammed in his face.

He hung his head so that his hat blocked out any view of Jana walking away from him. If only he could have—

A startled cry had him looking up again quickly. Jana had climbed halfway into the helicopter.

Her right arm flailed as she fell backward. He looked up in time to see her try to save herself by grabbing the edge of the doorframe with her good hand, but momentum ripped her fingers free.

He took one step. Two…

But he was too late, Jana went down hard. Her metal hooks made a sharp grinding as they skidding across the pavement when she tried to stave off the fall.

Her head hit with a sickening thud. She groaned once and, going limp, lay still.

"Shit!" Jasper dropped to his knees beside her, but didn't know what to do. "Curt! Anyone!" He screamed the last, but couldn't look up.

He reached for her twice, but couldn't complete the gesture. Then he remembered his basic CPR training.

No sign of blood spreading over the pavement. Check.

Breathing? He noted the rise and fall of her chest through the thin t-shirt she wore. Definitely breathing. Check. *Now look the hell away, man!*

He reached for her wrist…but it was made of plastic. Her flesh arm was twisted behind her back, though the angle didn't look weird or anything.

Jasper rested his hand on the curve over her throat. Not how he'd pictured their first ever touch. Jana's skin was incredibly smooth and soft. He felt the first beat of her pulse when someone suddenly knelt on Jana's other side.

Then a fist plowed into Jasper's jaw.

It was a good hit and sent him flying backward.

"What the hell did you do to her?" Curt screamed at him. "Why have you always hated her so much?"

He opened his mouth, but his jaw hurt like hell.

"You're an idiot, Curt," Stacy spoke up for him. "He doesn't hate Jana. He loves her."

He thought only *he* knew. He'd guarded the secret for so long that he couldn't answer now that it was out in the world. Now he could only close his eyes and bow his head.

He did love Jana. And didn't that just totally suck for him.

5

Jana woke slowly with her head nestled cozily in someone's lap. It was warm there. Safe.

The roar of a diesel engine was distant. Muted.

A cool hand rested for a moment on her forehead. She didn't remember taking a lover to bed last night. She hadn't taken one in a long, long time that she could recall.

There was a hard jostle, enough to make her head explode with pain. She might not see stars, but she felt as if she'd been hit by a nebula, maybe an entire galaxy.

"Shh, Jana. We're almost there."

She risked opening one eye and squinted up at Stacy's breasts. A slight shift of focus and she saw her face looking down worriedly.

"Where…" was all she managed in a dry croak.

"Back of one of our pickup trucks. Almost to the hospital."

"You're not driving," Jana could hear the racing

engine. Stacy was notorious as the only member on the team who always drove exactly on the speed limit.

"Maggie is. We wanted to get you there this century," Stacy half smiled and then smoothed her hand over Jana's forehead again.

"Wha—"

Maggie must have jumped a curb the size of an aircraft hangar—the jumbo jet size. Her world exploded in a flash of white pain.

"Easy, Maggie," Stacy called out loudly enough to make Jana cringe.

She tried to cover her ears. One side worked. On the other side all she did was ram her hooks into Stacy's side.

"Hey!" Stacy grunted out.

"Sorry. Pothole," Maggie called from the front. "They grow them big around here."

"What hap—" Jana tried again but could only squeeze her eyes tight as they slewed around a corner like a banking Sikorsky Black Hawk under heavy fire.

"Missed that one," Maggie called out happily.

"We're not sure," Stacy was looking down at her steadily, as if the truck wasn't on an insane roller coaster ride.

"You were talking to Jasper when I turned my back. Next thing I know you're flat on the ground and Jasper is kneeling over you freaking out and crying for help. He said you ran into a helicopter."

She'd run into something. Hard. She'd been too… something to see what it was. All Jana remembered was the helpless flail as both her hand and her hooks failed her. She'd—they slammed over another bump.

"That one *was* a curb. Sorry," Maggie spoke up.

Jana remembered losing her balance, but that was the last thing. "Must have fallen and knocked myself out."

"By the size of the lump on your head, we were thinking that you ran at the helo headfirst with all your might."

"Lump?" She reached for it.

"Hey! Hey! Cut that out," there was a pressure on her arm. Stacy was fending off Jana's right arm and hooks.

"Sorry," she tried again with the left and couldn't stop the hiss of pain when she found the bump. "Oh my god. That's huge!"

"Hence the race to the hospital."

"And...we're here!" Maggie slammed on the big truck's brakes hard enough to chirp the tires and almost enough to tumble Jana out of Stacy's lap and onto the backseat's floor.

Jana tried to sit up, but Stacy used that cool hand on her forehead to keep her in place.

"Don't you dare. Now lie still. You sit up and puke all over this truck, we're going to leave it for you to clean up. You puke on me and you might have to find yourself a new sister-in-law."

"Okay, Stacy."

And she lay there, oddly at peace with her head in Stacy's lap. Being taken care of. It wasn't something she was used to, but Stacy's inner kindness made it easy to accept.

Taken care of.

She'd been protesting about just that to someone recently.

Telling someone…no, *yelling* at someone that she didn't need that. This. But she liked this.

The door next to Stacy opened and a pair of blue-gloved hands held either side of her head as Stacy slid out. Then they placed a board beneath her before they eased her out the door and onto a rolling gurney.

"All I did was bump my head." Then her head hit the soft pillow and she yelped. One side might be soft, but someone must have hidden a brick under the other side.

"Easy," the blue-gloved doctor said. "I don't want to turn your head until we've checked out there are no neck injuries."

Jana was good with that. More than once she'd seen a helo pilot coming off a crash landing with a broken back. Please don't let her have that now. Please not that too.

So she lay on the gurney keeping her thoughts to herself as they slid a strap over her forehead and another across her shoulders. She missed Stacy's cool hand.

That's when she remembered why she'd run into the helicopter.

She'd been yelling at…Jasper.

Jana closed her eyes and groaned.

"How badly does it hurt?" Stacy asked as she crushed Jana's one hand in both of hers.

It hurt bad. The things she'd said to Jasper…

Why couldn't she have kept *those* thoughts to herself?

6

"Nuh-uh. I know that look."

"What look?" Jasper couldn't turn to face Curt. All he could see was the cloud of dust Maggie had left as she'd raced away toward the hospital.

"That I'm-going-to-leave-and-never-come-back look. I saw Palo try that on Maggie. I get it now."

Palo spoke up from his other side, "Don't do it, bro. The payoff ain't there. I'm telling you."

Jasper watched the dust that refused to settle in the baking twilit air. Everything was smudged and dirty. His hands from working over a fire all day. The sky. All of his dreams.

"I'm not gonna let you," Curt was still on old news.

Jasper turned to Palo. "Where is the payoff then?"

"Hitting the homerun," Curt could be a peacock strutting his shit. Now he and Palo both ignored him.

Jasper waited while Palo chewed on his answer. Curt finally caught on and kept his yap shut until Palo was ready to speak.

"Don't take 'no' for an answer," he finally offered.

"It was a mighty thorough, in-my-face 'no' to be ignoring."

"Then man up!" Curt's answer to almost everything, but Palo nodded his agreement. Curt and Stacy had been such an obvious fit from the first moment, that it seemed there'd been no other possibility. Palo'd had his work cut out for him to win Maggie's heart, yet he'd pulled it off. Maybe Jasper should trust him.

He pulled out his keys and headed for his Camaro.

"Oh no you don't!" Curt grabbed his arm.

Jasper's jaw still hurt like hell and he could feel the pressure of the swelling around his eye. He considered returning the favor, but couldn't think of any reason to do so. Curt had just been defending Jana, something Jasper had been trying to do his entire life.

Jasper yanked his arm free. "I'm going to the hospital to check on her. That's all."

"Then I'm coming with you."

"Fine."

"Fine?" Curt clearly didn't believe him. Not that Jasper cared. As long as Curt didn't remember what Stacy had said about Jasper's true feelings. How the hell had she known anyway?

"Fine. Get in the car," and Jasper climbed into his black-and-flame painted Camaro. He looked back at Palo, "You coming?"

Palo shook his head. "Maggie would kill me if I left with her helos unsecured."

Jasper nodded. The man knew his woman. Then he and Curt rolled out the front gate and headed for the hospital which lay just four miles away through town.

Curt let the first three-point-eight go by in silence, then asked, "Since when have you loved Jana?"

Jasper focused on the last two-tenths as he rolled into the hospital parking lot and found a spot close by the Firebirds' big, black Denali pickup. Jasper closed his eyes and leaned back in his seat, keeping his hands on the wheel.

"Well?"

He sighed, but finally answered. "Since the first moment I saw her."

"You were six."

"So were you."

"Sis was ten."

"She was."

Curt started to laugh.

Jasper glared over at him.

"Got a thing for older women, do you?"

Jasper debated if it was enough reason to hit his best friend—at least a knuckle punch on the nerve center in his upper arm. But he couldn't find the motivation.

"Only since I was six," he got out of the car and went to find Jana.

# 7

"We're keeping you overnight," the civilian doctor actually tried to sound soothing which was better than most Army docs managed. "Gave yourself a hell of a whack there and a moderate concussion."

Not being a stupid doctor, he also retreated before Jana could manage more than a feeble protest. They'd given her a prescription strength Tylenol, but it didn't seem to be doing anything for the steady thud of the headache emanating from the lump on the back of her head.

Maggie and Stacy came up to either side of her bed the moment the doctor cleared out.

"It sounds good," Stacy had been hanging out with her brother too much. She had become almost as matter-of-fact as Curt. Or had she been that way from the beginning?

"Good?" Jana protested.

"You aren't dead, honey," Maggie brushed Jana's hair away from her face.

"A blessing of small favors," she closed her eyes. She was glad she was mostly uninjured. The only part of her that she wished was dead at the moment was the part that had told Jasper to go to hell for being nice to her.

"What?" Stacy took her hand and held it. That made her aware that her other hand had been removed and was sitting on the side table. It took her a couple of tries, and some embarrassing help from Maggie, to get her stump out of sight beneath the sheet. Even that grated at her, though it was a simple kindness. Had she so isolated herself from everyone?

"I said awful things to Jasper. Things he didn't deserve. At least I don't think so. It's all muddled up. Anyway, I totally screwed up everything, as usual."

"You're not the only one," Stacy's voice was laced with enough chagrin to make Jana open her eyes once more. Stacy seemed to take a sudden interest in a heart monitor that wasn't showing anything, because the doctor hadn't turned it on. The only sound in the room was the air conditioning and the quiet chatter of a couple nurses at their station down the hall.

"Spill it."

"Uh…"

Jana risked moving her head to check on Maggie, but she was watching Stacy with wide eyes. Curiosity… or not believing that Stacy was about to reveal some dark secret? Jana couldn't tell.

"Stacy?"

"I…might have…said something. Something that maybe I shouldn't."

"What? To who?"

"To Curt."

"What did you say to my brother?"

"That…" Now Stacy was taking an interest in the ceiling tiles. When she went to step away, Jana held her hand tighter, even giving it a slight yank to make Stacy look at her. The gesture was a mistake, as at the moment everything in her body seemed to be connected to the throbbing lump on the back of her head.

"Stacy…"

Stacy blushed bright pink to the ears.

"I said—"

"There she is! Hey, Sis," Curt's voice boomed into the room, almost splitting Jana's head in two.

She winced until the pressure wave of the sound blast stopped echoing inside her head. When her eyes were able to refocus, she saw that someone was hiding behind Curt.

It wasn't working.

Her brother might be six-foot tall and have broad shoulders that Stacy couldn't help gushing about. But the lean man hiding behind him was six-foot-three and was topped by another several inches of cowboy hat.

"Get out!" Now her own voice was hurting her head.

The visible part of the cowboy hat turned for the door.

"No! Not you, Jasper. Everyone else, out. Now."

"But…" Stacy held onto her hand.

Jana squeezed it briefly, then let go. "Shoo," she whispered it softly.

"Buddy!" Curt slapped Jasper on the shoulder hard enough to send him stumbling into a wall. He turned to Jana, "You wouldn't believe what he said about—"

Jasper grabbed him by the wrist, flipped it up behind Curt's back hard enough to make him squeak in pain, before Jasper shoved him out the door hard enough that he almost hit the wall on the other side of the hall.

It took some cajoling to get the women to leave. Enough that Jana was beginning to wonder just how blind she'd been about Maggie's and Stacy's loyalty to her. They kept trying to hover, even when she didn't want them to. She apparently had real friends, despite how she brushed people off.

Stacy patted Jasper on the shoulder as she left. Maggie, who was over a foot shorter, pulled him down to kiss him on the cheek.

As the room cleared, she wondered how in the world she was going to take back the things she'd said to Jasper. She'd meant…some of it. But not all. She could feel a whirling mix of fear that Jasper would decide to leave the Firebirds and joy that he was here in her hospital room. The two combined to leave her feeling rather nauseated despite the drugs the doctor had given her for just that.

At last it was just them, though she could hear the others clustered outside the door having a whispered conversation.

At her signal, Jasper closed the door.

"Jasper, I…" No, she was being a coward, staring at the white ceiling. She turned to look directly at him. "Jasper, I… What the hell happened to your face?" One cheek and eye were purpling badly and the eye was half swollen shut.

"Your brother," he spoke barely above a mumble.

"Curt punched you?"

"I suppose that for a moment he thought I was the one who'd knocked you out. He's even more protective of you than I am. You hit the ground hard. Scared me halfway back to Texas. Guess you scared him worse and he saw me kneeling over you with my hand at your throat."

"At my throat?" Jana swallowed her throat suddenly felt dry.

"I was trying to make sure you had a pulse."

"A pulse?"

Jasper nodded.

"And that prompted the longest sentence you've ever spoken to me."

Jasper shrugged.

"Why do you hate me so much?"

"I don't."

And he was right. A man who hated her wouldn't rescue her by taking her out running. A man who hated her wouldn't think up something as elegant as the Firebirds to give her a purpose when her parents were gone and she'd needed one so desperately.

"Okay…" She thought about it a minute. "Then why don't you ever speak to me?"

8

"Because I..." Jasper desperately wanted to admit to being an idiot and then walk away while he still could. But that sounded even lamer than the truth.

Jana waited for him.

To buy himself a moment, he poured her a paper cup of water from a small carafe. But there was no straw for her to drink it while she was lying down, so he drank it himself. Then tried to figure out what to do with the little cup. Not the sharps bin. Not...

He set it on the white steel table by the carafe and her disconnected arm. It was strange seeing the hooks without her attached.

Forcing himself, he turned to her. By her perfect stillness it was obvious how much she was hurting. He could also see by the lines of the thin white sheet that she wore nothing other than an even thinner hospital gown beneath that. There was an extra bit of flatness along her right side where the hooks should be.

Over the years he'd seen Jana looking elegant in a

prom dress or hot in a swimsuit—thankfully she'd favored one-pieces over bikinis or it might have killed him. In full military dress, she'd been imposing. In casual camp gear, she'd been a treat.

But lying here, he was forced to take a step closer.

"Is it hard being back in a hospital?"

Her darting look away told him just how hard. She actually shivered.

He took the blanket from the foot of her bed and spread it over her. He pulled up a chair by her bedside and waited her out.

She finally nodded, but still didn't look at him.

"I'm sorry I made you so angry."

"Maybe…I shouldn't have been," she stayed focused on the far wall.

"Would it have helped if I'd told you the things I was planning back when I was planning them?"

"Duh," and she moved enough to stare at the white fluorescent ceiling fixture for a while. At length, she finally looked at him. "Though to be honest, maybe not. If you'd told me you were taking me out running because I was busy making myself even more depressed with each passing day, I might have force fed you my sneakers."

"And the Firebirds?"

"I don't know. It was so elegant. It saved me. It saved both of us. It got Curt in charge of his own company, which he always wanted. It got him Stacy which is a gift beyond any he ever dreamed of."

Jasper knew that. He'd seen his best friend come to life from the moment they met. He knew what that felt like, deep inside. Every time Jana brushed against his life

—even just a quick overseas text to Curt that was mentioned in passing—had breathed life into him.

"If you'd told me, would I have believed in it any less? Would I have worked any less hard to make it happen? I don't know."

"You liked that it was for your family. For you and Curt."

"I did," Jana nodded, with only a small wince of pain this time.

Jasper had known that about her. However much she'd complained about her little brother while they were growing up, the love was there like a shining streak of sunlight.

"I'd lost all hope after I did this," she raised her right arm and it slipped clear of the sheets. "You found a way to give that back to me."

He'd never seen her stump before. Jana Williams was *never* in public without her arm on. Even in the early days, when he knew it was hurting her, she wouldn't take it off.

He'd almost expected something hideous with how she hid it so carefully. But it looked as natural as could be. He couldn't even see any scars at the end. Her arm simply tapered to a stubby point, a little wider than the bone that still remained within.

She saw where he was looking and tried to tuck it back out of sight.

Before she could, he simply lay his hand on the remaining upper part of her forearm, to show her it was okay.

## 9

Jana's breath caught in her throat.

*No one* touched her arm. The last person had been an Army physical therapist three years ago.

But Jasper's hand lay upon her skin as calmly as if it was the most normal thing in the world. She could feel herself switch from frozen stiff to blind panic.

"Easy, Jana. Just breathe. Okay? Just breathe."

And somehow, his hand, lying so casually upon her hideous stub, let her do that. Let her breathe.

Jasper sighed. "The reason I don't talk to you?"

She nodded, welcoming any distraction. His fingers began tracing lightly over her skin. Small movements, so tiny they probably weren't conscious. But they stroked the skin by her elbow as if it was just…skin. Such a strange feeling.

"You were always so out of reach. Too old when I was kid. Then married to your job and engaged to Captain What's His Name."

Captain What's His Name had never been her

fiancé. He was gay as could be. But they'd become super close friends. She'd been his excuse to avoid the harassment that still existed in so many places, including his own family so he'd taken his leaves with her instead of going home. He'd been her shield against unwelcome advances. He'd kept promising to come visit her—she was the one who'd told him no and shut him out. Apparently he had also been a signal to Jasper to steer clear.

"Once you were injured and he dropped you…" She could hear the fury in Jasper's voice.

"He didn't."

"You're still engaged?" Jasper jerked his hand away from her arm. She missed it. And she liked that he would never even touch another man's woman, but it was clear that he wanted to touch her. Quite why was beyond her—did he really not see what a crippled wreck she was? But she wasn't going to be chasing him off anymore either.

"We never were. Different story for a different time."

Jasper looked thoughtful for a long moment, then slowly returned his hand to rest on her skin. This time, she was pretty sure that the gentle brushing of his fingertips was conscious.

"Once you got back, you were so…"

"I was so totally fucked up," Jana knew what she'd been.

"…down," Jasper concluded. "I wanted to help."

"Then what was with the silence thing?"

Jasper's fingers stopped and he looked down, his cowboy hat hiding his eyes.

"Jasper?" The silence stretched until she thought her head was going to crack.

"You already gave me your answer." He took his hand away and struggled to his feet. He turned for the door without looking at her.

"Jasper!"

He kept going.

"You turn around and set your ass right back in that chair. We're going to have this out now!" She'd sat up halfway, making the room spin. She flopped back down on the pillow and the pain bloomed to life—straight through the drugs. "Uh!" Jana could only grunt and squeeze her eyes shut while waiting for the spins and the pain to subside.

No hand returned to her arm, but after a long, whirling silence, she heard the slight scrape of the chair as Jasper settled back into it.

What was it that nobody wanted to tell her? Not Jasper. Not Maggie. Her brother had tried. Stacy had also tried—tried and failed. Something the doctor had told the others? But that didn't fit. She wiggled her toes and the fingers of her good hand to be sure. All accounted for.

She kept her eyes closed, the spins weren't quite gone yet.

"What did Stacy say to my brother?"

"She said that I loved you." Jasper said it flat out. No grumble or complaint. No sigh or hesitation.

Jana opened one eye and looked at him.

He was watching her from deep under the shadow of the cowboy hat's brim.

"And that meant that you'd never speak to me again?"

"I never spoke to you in the first place."

"Jasper!"

He groaned. "I was always scared shitless that you'd say 'no.' And *then* you *did.*"

She had, hadn't she. "I was angry."

"So angry that you fell out of a parked helicopter and knocked yourself out cold." And Jasper's smile came out. She'd seen it with Curt or when he was with the other guys. It had never been aimed at her before and it was a damned nice smile—even if he was teasing her. He *was* teasing her. That too was new.

"But—" Jana twitched her half-arm beneath his lingering hand. She was less than whole in so many ways.

"*That* doesn't have shit to do with who you are, Jana. I'm not that shallow. To my eyes, you're the most beautiful woman there is. If you think this changed that…" Jasper just shook his head sadly as he wrapped his fingers more tightly around the stub of her arm until he was holding it in a solid, intimate grip.

Jana had asked Curt once how he knew that Stacy was right for him. Even when pushed, his best answer had been that he "just knew."

Jana had never "just known" anything in her life.

Except maybe this one time she did.

Her phantom hand had gone quiet. No need to twitch her shoulder, click her hooks, or fool with her hair. Somehow, her missing hand was finally where it belonged—safe beneath Jasper's.

She slowly bent her half-arm toward herself. Jasper's grip held tight and he let the tension slowly draw him forward until his face was close by hers, under the shade of his cowboy hat.

He hesitated half an inch out, and she raised herself

up just enough to kiss him. It wasn't some mild, gentle, hesitant kiss.

Jasper knew who she really was. Apparently better than she did. And he made it abundantly clear that he wanted her exactly as she was. His kiss built like a wave under her skin until it flushed with imagination of what would happen as soon as she was out of this bed and in another one.

She'd been kissed plenty before…well, before. She'd let no man kiss her since the accident. Why would anyone want to? But amazingly one man did.

And maybe that one man was all she needed.

After he finally returned to the chair…

When her head stopped spinning from a hundred good reasons instead of one bad one…

While his hand still wrapped lightly about the stub of her arm more intimately than if they were holding hands…

Sleep began to slide over her. The emotional day, the concussion, everything. But there was one more question that had always bothered her.

"Jasper."

"Uh-huh."

"What's with the cowboy hat? You've been in Oregon since you were four."

"Six," but he chuckled. "Do you remember the first words you ever said to me?"

She tried to concentrate, but his kiss had left her in such a floaty, dreamy state that she couldn't seem to.

"It was on the day we moved in next door. First time I ever saw you, Jana."

"Sorry, I don't. Is that bad?"

"No. Not bad. It probably meant nothing to you. It changed my entire world."

"What was it?" Her eyes drifted shut, she couldn't fight off the sleep that overwhelmed her. It wasn't just the day and knocking herself out. It was also learning that this special man could love her just as she was—impossibly he saw her as whole. And now that he did, nothing else mattered. So many fears left behind. Without them she could see something she'd long forgotten—that the future was a place of hope. Even from that single kiss, some part of her *knew* that she'd walk beside this man for as long as they both should live. What girl didn't dream of that?

His lips brushed over hers once more, then he leaned in to whisper in her ear.

"You looked me square in the eye—you have such beautiful eyes, Jana—and you said, 'Nice hat.' I've worn one ever since just for you. I did all of it just for you."

# THEY BOTH HOLD THE TRUTH

***Ty Franks*** *works as handyman for the Firebirds. But all summer he lives a lie. When he rescues smokejumper Mallory Kerr, he must choose between his hidden truth and future happiness.*

***Mallory*** *lost friends and alienated family because she knows what she is meant to do—parachute to wildfire.*

*The fire between them burns, until her present truth collides head-on with his past secrets.*

# INTRODUCTION

Ty and Mallory posed a special challenge for me. I've written romances for characters from their mid-twenties to their sixties. I've written interracial love stories and adventures for young teens.

But! Writing about Ty and Mallory was a particular challenge. First, a bit of background as to what I found so challenging.

To me a romance means happily-ever-after (HEA). A romance story is about the one true love that we all hope for (even, or perhaps especially, when we don't believe it is really possible). There has been a trend of recent years, as the romance genre has so expanded, to include what is called "happily-for-now."

When *Bridget Jones's Diary* exploded chick lit onto the scene, it was bundled in with romances. And I took it as a romance…with a satisfying HEA—in the end Bridget gets the right man. When the sequel came out and revealed that it wasn't, I was hugely offended as a reader. I had bought into the HEA, only to have it ripped away. Some argue that it is more realistic, and perhaps it is.

## INTRODUCTION

But those are not the stories I wish to read or tell. (I'll just mention that I heaved the book across the room and never finished it.)

Now, back to Ty and Mallory. I had never set out to give an HEA to such a young couple. How to make that believable? How to make it so that it didn't happen too fast? Adults might be able to transition more believably from first meeting to true love with their more experienced and mature viewpoints. But how to make Ty and Mallory's journey believable…to me?

As I hope you'll see, I gave them their HEA—I *know* they'll be together when they're done—but I also gave them the time to discover the truth of it, rather than needing to realize that truth within the scope of the story.

There was a lot that I liked about this couple. They were from wildly different backgrounds in a curious way. Ty's background was internal to the Oregon Firebirds world. Mallory, however, had previously been with the Firehawks smokejumpers. In *Wildfire on the Skagit* (Firehawks Smokejumpers #3) she is a minor character who faces her inner demons. And in doing so, she helps the hero face his. (It is an incredibly touching scene that actually made me tear up all over again when I reread it prior to writing this story.)

I appreciate the Firebirds versus Firehawks contrast that dynamic brought to the story. And I loved the challenge of giving someone as cool as Mallory a love story no matter her age.

1

Ty had trouble keeping his attention on the road. The steeply-jagged peaks of the Selway-Bitterroot Wilderness towered close over either side of Montana's Highway 93 and he kept hunching over the wheel to crane upward. He'd traveled this road a hundred times growing up, but a summer of working for the Oregon Firebirds had given him a whole new calibration for how rugged it was.

As he raced along—the third pickup in a line of three—Ty Franks decided that it had been a near perfect summer in ways he'd never expected. And definitely nothing like he'd planned.

Getting hired by the Firebirds as a Ty-of-all-trades handyman had always been his plan. He had to find out all he could about the owners Curt and Jana Williams—brother and sister. But he'd had fun with the team which was a complete and unexpected bonus. A bonus that was fast becoming a burden.

Despite being just a summer hire, the Firebirds team had tried to make him one of their own. They'd certainly welcomed him as if he had always been. And, now that the summer was ending and the northern fire season was drawing to a close, he wished that he'd let them.

Instead, he'd done his best to keep his distance. A distance that was about to grow. The team headed south to fight the inevitable Southern California fires. And he was headed back to school (at least until the University of Montana in Missoula found out he was broke and that he didn't really care about any of their coursework anyway).

Over the last four months he'd willingly helped Jana with operations paperwork and team logistics.

Maggie had taught him the basics of maintaining the helicopters from refueling to checking air filters. By the end of the summer, she trusted him with hydraulics, greasing joints, and a dozen other tasks—both messy and not. She always doublechecked him, because that's the kind of mechanic she was, but she didn't let the pilots do a tenth of the things she'd taught him. When she'd torn apart each of the turbine engines as part of a duty-cycle service, she'd let him be her assistant—like his mom being an OR nurse before she died. He'd handed Maggie tools and parts and asked a thousand questions—that she'd always answered in that cheerful way she had. It had been awesome.

He'd never done long-haul trucking, but he'd grown a taste for it as one of the Firebirds' drivers. The team had three big Denali pickups, each rigged to tow a low-boy trailer with a pair of MD 520N firefighting helicopters strapped on. Within a day, they'd been able to place all six of the helos almost anywhere in the West.

They'd fought fires from San Francisco to the Canadian border, from the Oregon Coast over to Idaho.

Right now, by some random chance, they were heading home. He'd grown up in Missoula, Montana, and attended—had attended—university there. His past lay less than an hour ahead, yet it felt like the most foreign place ever. He had no Mom, she'd told him Dad had died in a car wreck when Ty was two, and soon no school. His worldly belongings were in a pack in the back of the truck.

Seeking any distraction, he looked up again at the cloud of smoke. The dirty snarl of ash, bigger than any thunderhead, reached all the way up to the jet stream where it was a sheared-off flattop. Three months ago he'd have thought nothing of it, just some distant storm cloud. Now he knew that was true, but it was a *fire* storm cloud made of smoke. And by the size and color of the column it was big and burning incredibly hot to lift dark ash that high.

He considered waking up Drew and Amos to point it out, but they'd be getting little enough sleep in the next few days as pilots. The other pilots were probably passed out in their own trucks as he, Maggie, and Jana raced them and their helos toward the fire.

It had been funny watching the crew pair off through the summer—and not just for some quick sex. They were engaged, talking weddings. It was weird. Also strange: it hadn't changed who rode with who. Curt, the team's leader, always rode with his sister, Jana. Another pilot Palo always rode with them. And that was despite Curt marrying Stacy and the impending weddings of Palo to Maggie, and Jana to Jasper. It was hard not to envy them. Sure, the women were all much older than he was—late twenties, even thirties—but they were some seriously hot women.

All the couples had been scattered across the trucks for the long drives at the start of the summer. They'd decided to stay that way even after they got together. Maybe they thought it made for happy marriages or some other equally dumb fantasy. Going through his mom's stuff, he'd learned that was all a lie.

"Leaves just us three single guys to whine together," Ty mouthed one of Drew's favorite complaints on his sleeping friend's behalf.

Friends, that was another thing he'd never expected to find among the Oregon Firebirds, but he had. It was easy to see himself hanging with Drew and Amos… except he was almost done with the Firebirds. He'd even toyed with the idea of changing his major from law to forestry, because law was sure as hell a yawner. It was pointless as he'd have to drop out anyway, just like he had last year when Mom got so sick, but—*Shit!*

*That* got his determination back on track. The Firebirds might think they were nearly done with him, but he was a long way from being done with them. Ty gripped the steering wheel until his knuckles went white and it became hard to steer along the winding two lane. Their parents might be dead too, but the brother and sister had yet to answer for their father.

But if Ty had let himself, sure he could have had fun. Gone to the bar with them, because he had the fake ID to match his summer alias.

*Nope!* It hadn't matched his plans.

But he was surprised to discover that he wished he had gone anyway.

2

Mallory Kerr dangled in the trees and debated between screaming and cursing. She had to choose soon, because otherwise she'd start crying—which wasn't ever on her agenda. Not even when her wrist hurt like…well, wildfire.

"What are you doing up there?"

"Enjoying the view," she snapped back over the radio. She finally spotted Krista standing in the dry-grass clearing wearing full smokejumper gear, wrestling her chute into a stuff sack. As she watched, the second stick of jump buddies—Evan and Akbar—floated into the clearing as if it was the easiest thing in the world.

"Okay, let me rephrase. Why aren't you doing anything about it?" The tiny Krista far below didn't even turn to look up—she just knew.

"The view is pretty," Mallory told her partner, even if she hadn't looked around at it yet. Humor, there was a path away from screaming, cursing, *or* crying and she took it. "And I screwed up my wrist."

The tiny figure far below stopped with all the chute

packing then shaded her eyes to really look up at Mallory. When she pulled out her binoculars, Mallory started feeling less comfortable—like a squirrel in a tree.

"Huh!" Krista's grunt didn't make her feel much better.

Looking away, Mallory did finally see the view, which was stunning—one of the things she loved about smokejumping. She'd always liked the outdoors, but now she lived in it—had a job saving it.

The sharp mountain slopes of the Selway-Bitterroot Wilderness soared around her. Douglas fir stood proudly above tangled ranks of scrub alder and stone outcroppings. The clearing she'd been aiming for had been so close, but the capricious fire-driven wind had backed at the wrong moment and stolen most of her lift. She dropped vertically faster than any elevator, even flying briefly backwards. That's when she'd been slammed into this tree and snagged her chute.

Keeping her injured hand tight against her chest, she swung out a leg and then kicked it around like a ballet spin. Despite the harness she dangled from facing her outwards, she was able to twist enough to see what she'd landed in.

"Oh crap!" Mallory now saw what had earned her Krista's grunt. She'd managed to catch her parachute on an old king of the forest—on its very thinnest and uppermost branches.

Then she made the mistake of looking straight down as the harness spun her to face away from the tree once more. Heights never bothered her, at least not while the parachute was flying, but she was a long way up, on a very dead tree. Each breath she took might have enough force to snap the tip in two and dash her down to the forest floor. Because of how she'd snagged, she was about ten feet out into space from the trunk.

She didn't dare try pumping herself back and forth like a swing to reach the trunk. The slim treetop didn't even have a handy branch to grab and pull herself in. There was also no question of anyone climbing the tree to get to her—not unless they both wanted to die.

Looking down once more, she saw Krista hauling climbing gear out of her bag, even as the other smokies stopped her. It was suicide to climb up, but it took both of them to argue Krista out of trying anyway. Mallory knew she'd do the same—she'd do anything for Krista.

They'd met three years ago at a three-day smokejumpers adventure camp Krista had organized for high school girls. It had changed the direction of her life—as in she finally had one. In the two years she'd been jumping with Krista and the Mount Hood Aviation smokies, she'd only snagged one other tree—one of the best jump records in the entire team. That one she'd been able to climb down from without even needing a line. This one was going to suck.

"Can you at least get a line around the trunk?" Krista asked after the others had finally stopped her efforts.

Mallory had a hundred feet of 9mm climbing line coiled in the calf pouch of her Kevlar jumpsuit, on the same side as her bunged up wrist. She managed to snag one end of it with an awkward mid-air kneel and cross-reach. And there she hung, stupidly holding one end of the line in her only good hand, completely unable to see the trunk. Normally, she could tie on a small grapple, toss it over a branch, and pull herself in. But in her mind's eye she could still see the smooth, branchless expanse of this section of trunk. Nothing to hook onto.

*Not good!*

Again the need to scream surged into her hard enough to force a few tears from her eyes when she wouldn't give it a voice.

*Be calm. Be rational.* She went back over her training.

The only other real option was a direct lowering, tying off to the upper parachute harness, then releasing from it and descending. A hundred feet of line wouldn't get her out of a two hundred-foot tree—especially not one-handed.

"Just wait a moment," Krista thankfully called over the radio before Mallory could reconsider the screaming-cursing-crying emotional triangle.

Not willing to risk another twist, Mallory looked as far as she could north and south—she had a clear view of west. No sign of the fire, which meant it was directly behind her. That got her thinking about the heat-fuel-oxygen *fire* triangle. It was a baking hot summer with a fire coming over the ridge.

They'd jumped well ahead of it, enough to have time to prepare a fire break. But was it far enough? Other than Krista, the ground team—which had been augmented by more sticks of jumpers—were in full-hustle mode. But there was no way to gauge anything from that—smokies *lived* in full-hustle mode. Another thing she'd liked about jumping fires.

The air in the Selway-Bitterroot Wilderness was so fresh (except for the increasing smoke) that it might as well be pure oxygen. And fuel—she was perched two hundred feet up a tree so dead that it had shed its bark, leaving behind a weathered gray patina. About the best fuel there was and it would burn incredibly hot. The moisture in her body wouldn't be much more than a puff of steam if the tree caught fire while she was still in it.

"Help is coming," Krista called. "Just hang in there."

"Oh, like I have a choice." Mallory—or at least her imagination—could already feel the heat at her back.

3

The line of pickups suddenly jinked over to the side of the road and parked on the gravel shoulder. Ty kept his in the line, even though he didn't know what was going on. They were still thirty miles from Missoula. He nudged Drew and Amos awake.

"Something's up."

They blinked at him uncertainly.

"Ty, you're with me," Stacy grabbed his arm the second he stepped down from the truck and dragged him over to her helo. "Put this on."

Ty held the Nomex fire shirt and pants she'd thrown at him for a long moment. He'd gotten to go aloft on small flights with Maggie when she was testing the results of some of her maintenance work. He'd loved that. Helicopters were so cool. He'd never gotten to take a real flight and definitely not to anywhere he'd need protective gear.

But at the pace everyone was suddenly moving, there was no time to waste. He stripped and changed right there on the shoulder of Highway 93. He kept his head down so that no one could see his embarrassment at standing on a state highway wearing only briefs and a vintage Maroon 5 t-shirt that his mom had gotten years ago. He'd needed the added strength to face returning to the dead end of Missoula. Of course, right now, everything in his life was a dead end, which sucked beyond the depths of suckitude.

*Stay focused. Get dressed instead of standing half-naked in the middle of the highway.*

It normally took three people fifteen minutes to unload a helo from the lowboy trailer, unfold its rotors, and prepare it for flight. Within seconds, the entire team was grouped around Stacy's helo.

Drew and Amos were sent out in either direction to stop traffic. Everyone else got the machine unloaded onto the highway and fully prepped in under five minutes while people climbed out of their cars to gawk.

Stacy pointed at a headset and shoved him toward the backseat, which didn't seem much fun. The backseat of a firefighting MD 520N wasn't set up for comfort. It didn't even *have* seats—making the backseat phrase kinda pointless. Two seats equaled another five gallons of water-carrying capacity, so they'd been removed to save weight. And now they'd popped off the rear door leaving the rear area exposed to the world. In one corner of the back was a strapped down pile of fire gear: an emergency pack, a Pulaski fire axe, and some other things that he decided he'd rather not know the purpose of.

But, as everyone was in such a rush, he went where he was told. He barely had his safety line snapped in and headset on before Stacy had them aloft, taking off from the middle of Route 93. Before they disappeared out of sight below, he could see everyone else getting back in the trucks to continue toward Missoula.

There was an audience of over fifty cars watching them. He was down with that.

"Ty, we have a smokejumper snagged high in a tree," Stacy told him over the intercom headset. "No one else can get there as fast as we can, so it's up to us to fish them out."

Okay. That was cool enough to make him glad to sit on the cargo floor for his first real flight.

"Mine is the only Firebirds helo with a winch. You've got about six minutes to make sure you know how to work it. I can run it from here, but I'd rather pay attention to not getting us messed up with the fire."

"I've serviced this with Maggie," he let her know. Then went through it again just to be sure. He ran out ten feet of the steel wire, holding onto the snap hook at the end so that it didn't beat against the outside of the racing helo. Maggie would never forgive him if he scratched the paint on one of her precious birds. He reeled it back in.

"All good," he reported.

That was when he looked down. The terrain away from the highway was even rougher, almost brutal. He'd thought that the Siskiyou Mountains around the Firebirds' base in southwest Oregon were rugged. They were prairie lands compared to this.

Sharp peaks jagged upward out of the forest. The lower slopes were thick with trees except where long lines of bare rock showed winter avalanche scrapes. Perched atop one peak, he spotted a tiny lookout tower. He waved back at the couple watching him from the small hut atop the tall stilts.

It seemed like everyone was a couple, except for he, Drew, and Amos all relegated to their bachelor truck. Didn't matter. Not really. Even if it kinda did. He didn't believe in such shit, but they all made it look awfully—

Stacy's curse had him looking forward. Stacy never swore.

Glad that he'd kept his sunglasses, he leaned his face out into the wind through the open doorway. It only took a second to spot the black-and-red-flame parachute. It was snagged in the top of the tallest pine around—way at the top. If they screwed this up, the smokejumper was going to fall over two hundred feet and turn into a small, bloody patch on the rocks below.

Somehow it brought the whole summer into focus. He'd spent his days hanging around camp. Waiting for the helos to come back so that he could help clean them up and cram some calories into the pilots to get them back aloft. As for the fires, he'd only seen them from a distance or on the ground after they were burned out and the team was driving away.

Now they were flying toward an entire mountain sheathed in smoke and flames that reached twice the height of the trees. Even as he watched, a monster Canadair CL-415 water tanker flew in to dump water on the fire. He'd stood beside those at various airports over the summer—they were humungous. But on this fire, it looked like a tiny model plane dumping a Dixie cup of water on the massive conflagration.

"You fly into that?"

"Not unless we have to," Stacy replied. "The Firebirds are specialists in saving structures: homes, barns, businesses. We typically leave the monster wildfires for the big boys whenever we can. Though we've killed a lot of spot fires around the main firefight when we're called into the fray. Get the winch going."

He spooled it down as Stacy slowed and maneuvered above the trapped smokejumper. Ty kept an eye on the drum. Maggie had told him to never run it all the way out, but to always keep a few wraps of the wire on the drum for extra safety. He was the one who'd thought up painting the last ten feet bright red which had earned him a hard hug. It was quick—and she was older and engaged to Palo who could probably beat up Ty with his pinkie—but…damn!

"That's it," he announced as the first of the red spooled out and he stopped the winch. He then rested a hand on the wire to try and damp out the swinging motion.

"Let me bring it to the smokie," Stacy slowed even more. "If you try to swing it to them, we could snag a branch or miss completely."

So he concentrated on just keeping it steady as Stacy maneuvered them in above the smokejumper. He could see a cluster of a dozen more smokies who had now formed up in the clearing below. Even as he watched, they began cutting down the trees. Two fell almost simultaneously—well away from the one with the smokie caught in its branches. Though Ty could see them glancing aloft as they moved to the next trees.

He was on display. Center stage. And whatever anger he felt toward the owners of the Firebirds, he really didn't want to screw up.

# 4

Mallory watched the approaching helo from one direction. The rapidly thickening smoke from behind. And her jump team shifting into action below.

"Wish I was with you guys." Because if she was, she wouldn't be dangling up here with her wrist swelling painfully against the glove and cuff of her jump gear. She considered easing it, but even the thought of touching it sent shivers through her. Shivers that she hoped the dead tree didn't pick up on and decide it was time to snap off. Besides, if it was a bad break, the cuff might be the only thing stabilizing her wrist.

She could feel the downdraft of the helo's rotor blades wash over her and she just prayed that they didn't drive her out of the tree.

The wire cable flashed by fifty feet from her. That wasn't going to help at all, but she did her best to keep her eyes on it. She considered lifting her wire jump mask to get a better view, but decided to leave it in place so that she didn't get face-lashed by the swinging cable.

The next time it was only twenty feet away when it flashed by going the other way.

Ten and moving slower.

Five.

She lunged for it at three, which was a mistake. Because she was dangling, the lunge caused her body to twist out of the way. Then there was a sickening moment of weightlessness as one of the branches holding her parachute gave way. She dropped five feet before it caught again. A broken branch thudded off her jump helmet before it disappeared below. "So long, pal. Hope I don't see you soon."

Mallory had also lost sight of the cable.

It slapped hard against her bad wrist and she couldn't fight the scream of pain. She instinctively wrapped her good arm over her bad wrist to protect it and by pure luck, pinned the cable against her body.

The hook. How far down was the hook?

She very carefully trapped the cable against her body with her bad arm and began yanking it upward with her good hand. Ten feet. Twenty. At twenty-five she had the hook. Another instant and she had it securely snapped into the big D-ring on the front of her harness. Her heartrate decelerated from blind panic to mere overdrive. Overdrive she could deal with.

Mallory held her arms straight out to either side, ignoring the shooting pain of her unsupported wrist so that they'd know she was clear to lift.

It took forever, but the slack came out of the winch cable. They eased her out and away from the tree. The pressure came off the parachute harness. Then there was a sharp yank where the parachute attached at her shoulders. It flipped her upside down.

She slapped for the main chute cutaway.

Even as she yanked the double cord, dangling feet to the sky, she could see her parachute, snarled in the broken-off top of the tree, plummeting downward.

The triple-ring attachment released and she sprang upward against the helo's pull. Bouncing hard several times before she once more flipped right side up. Her bad hand got pinned between the winch cable and her chest.

She heard the start of her own scream, but thankfully passed out before she could hear the end of it.

# 5

"You stick with him until his own people arrive." Stacy was landing them gently on the giant green shamrock that marked the rooftop helipad of the St. Patrick Hospital in downtown Missoula. Ty could see a medical team waiting nearby with a gurney.

"Her," he managed to croak out.

"What's that?"

"Never mind. I'll stick."

He'd winched the unconscious smokejumper aloft as Stacy had raced toward the hospital. With no spare room, he'd dragged the smokie into his lap. He'd left the winch cable attached to the smokie's harness and wrapped his arms around both the harness and the jumpsuit for stability during the wild flight around the bucking fire winds.

That's when he'd learned just how much of the person's bulk was jumpsuit and how little of it was smokejumper.

A peek through the wire mesh on the front of the helmet revealed a pale, slender face, and a long loop of white-blonde hair.

The smokejumper was a she. He took the liberty of swinging up her mask to make sure she was still breathing. Her face wasn't pretty, it was gorgeous. Like model gorgeous. Prettier than any girl guys like him ever got to hold—even when passed out in full smokejumper gear.

He'd nearly choked when their helicopter had briefly been dragged downward by the broken treetop snarled in the jumper's parachute. After she'd released it, he'd only been able to watch in horror as treetop and parachute plummeted into the towering forest below while the smokejumper's body had bounced and flipped at the end of his winch cable like a broken doll.

She was breathing. And beautiful. And young. How could a girl his own age be out doing something as wild as jumping into a wildfire? All he'd done all summer was push papers and polish helicopter windscreens. While she'd been... It was just crazy.

The moment Stacy touched the helo's skids down on the pad, the medical team raced forward, ducking below the spinning rotors. In seconds they had her removed from his lap, on the gurney, and were headed for the elevator.

"Go!" Stacy shouted over the intercom.

Ty lunged forward, and was slammed back into place by his safety line.

Free of that, he was nearly decapitated by the intercom headset, then tangled with the winch hook. He managed to get the former into the pocket on the back of the pilot's seat and snapped the latter onto the keeper loop. He could hear Stacy laughing at him as he sprinted away. He barely cleared the closing doors as he dodged sideways into the elevator.

"You next of kin?" One of the nurses confronted him as he stumbled for balance, trying not to faceplant atop the smokie still out cold on the gurney.

"Rescue team."

She didn't look impressed.

"I've been ordered to stick with my teammate." The last bit was a bald lie but, like so much of his summer, it was a plausible one.

The nurse finally nodded and turned back to their charge.

Again he was almost left behind when the door on the back side of the elevator was the one that opened.

"What can you tell us?"

"She got her parachute snagged in a treetop."

But what was wrong with her? She'd been conscious when she'd latched herself onto the cable. Then he pictured the painstaking way she'd worked with the cable while he'd held his breath until he could feel himself turning blue.

"Not sure about everything, but there's definitely something with her…" he closed his eyes for a moment to concentrate on the whirl of images, "…left wrist or arm."

They rolled her into an exam room.

One of the attendees probed one arm and then the other. The left one earned the nurse a yelp of pain.

"Ow! Don't touch!"

The smokejumper was suddenly wide awake and

staring straight at him with the bluest eyes he'd ever seen.

"Who are you?"

The nurse turned to glare at him.

*Crap!*

# 6

Mallory hadn't been in a hospital except once. Her best friend Meaghan had gotten a bad cut windsurfing out on the Columbia Gorge and needed nine stitches. Mallory had been with her and taken her to…she looked around…maybe this very room. A shocking change from falling out of a tree just a moment before.

She needed one of Meaghan's easy laughs right about now.

Except she was two years gone, off at the University of Washington in Seattle. At seventeen, Mallory had always thought they'd go to the same college, friends for life and all that. Now she was a much wiser twenty and knew that choices could separate people. No one—least of all her parents—understood her sudden change from ballet to smokejumping and forest ecology.

But *she* understood it and that was all that mattered.

"No! It's just my wrist," she protested when they wanted to cut away her Kevlar jumpsuit. It was stupid, but it was her first jumpsuit and it had lasted her for two seasons now. It was just a piece of Kevlar with pockets full of gear, but it was hers—a part of who she was now. No one had believed she could be a smokejumper other than Krista and Evan, her husband. Her parents still didn't. This suit was what had proved them all wrong.

The pain was horrific as they eased open the cuff and got her out of the jumpsuit. Then the Nomex fire shirt that she'd worn over her t-shirt.

To ignore the pain, she kept her attention on the gawky guy still standing at the foot of the bed. He had a thin face and dark eyes, which a sloppy hank of his thick brown hair partially obscured. Kinda broody and intense which she sort of liked.

The nurse was trying to shoo him out and he was edging back under protest. But he wasn't looking at the nurse, he was looking at her like she was some kind of miracle. He wore fire gear and it looked good on him, like it belonged. At the moment she'd gladly take a wildland firefighter over the rather scary doctor and two nurses.

"No, it's okay," she called out.

The nurse huffed out her frustration, but finally departed to other tasks. A bunged-up wrist apparently didn't need two nurses even if chasing off the only even partly familiar thing in the room did.

"Who are you?" Mallory had to focus on something as they prepared her for an x-ray.

"I'm Ba— I'm Ty. Ty Franks," he said it like he was trying to convince himself. "I was up in the helo. I ran the winch."

"Oh. Thanks for that."

He stuck with her through x-ray, doctor consult, a temporary splint, and release. They ended up together on the bench in the front of the hospital, with him hauling her jump gear around over one shoulder. It was a large, awkward mass weighing over fifty pounds—reserve chute plus enough food and gear to work on the fire line for days—but he didn't complain once.

Ty had also done his best to cheer her up as the doctor talked through the steps of recovery. A multiple "simple fracture"—it didn't feel simple. Ice the wrist. Aspirin or ibuprofen. A week in the splint while the swelling subsided, then six weeks in the cast. Done for the fire season. That last had been hard to take, but Ty had told her she was lucky that was all. He'd even made her laugh somehow about a busted wrist being better than becoming a tiny, Mallory-shaped blood splatter on rocks below that old-growth pine.

"Where can I take you?"

She didn't really know. "My jump team will still be in the firefight. Our helos are committed in Reno, Nevada right now. I think our hotshots are at a fire on Washington's Olympic Peninsula. I doubt if our plane pilots stuck around after we jumped."

"You could come hang with us."

"Us?" He hadn't said much except to ask how she was doing every thirty seconds—which was actually kind of sweet because he was so concerned. It had been a while since she'd gobsmacked a seriously cute boy into stuttering silence. Her fellow smokies were all multi-season veterans and much older than she was. The Hoodies—as Mount Hood Aviation's smokejumpers were known—had never taken a rookie, except for her. Mallory had become everyone's little sister on the team. She'd been her school's beauty queen, back when she thought that was important. It was kind of nice having someone see her as female again.

"The Oregon Firebirds. We've got six helos on site. I figured you'd need a ride, so I called them while you were checking out." Even as he said it, a big black GMC Denali pickup pulled up to the curb. Despite being burdened with her jump gear, he opened and held the front passenger door for her, before clambering in back.

She glanced over at the driver, but her eyes snagged where the woman's hand grabbed the steering wheel. Except it wasn't a hand, it was a pair of steel hooks.

"Hi, I'm Jana."

Mallory looked down at the splint and heavy wrapping around her left wrist. Ty hadn't been kidding. She'd been incredibly lucky. There was no way to be a smokejumper without both hands.

"Hi, I'm Jana," the woman repeated. There was a hint of a laugh as she reached over to lightly tap her hooks against Mallory's splint. The tiniest zing of pain knocked away her surprise.

"Sorry. I, uh—"

"Her name's Mallory," Ty rescued her. "She just found out she's out for the season. I guess it threw her for a loop."

"Kinda," was all she could think to say.

"Be glad that's all it is," Jana briefly flourished her hooks, then used them to drop the truck into gear as if it was the most natural thing in the world.

Six hours ago, everything had seemed so natural in Mallory's world. She was an MHA smokejumper—an elite job in a dangerous profession. She'd even jumped lead stick with Krista—who everyone agreed was absolutely awesome.

Now everything was unnatural, she had nowhere to belong, yet *she* was the lucky one. And she *was.* And even though part of her didn't feel that way, a part of her did.

She knew that was Ty's doing.

Mallory turned around to mouth a 'Thank you' to him. The words caught in her throat. He was staring at her again, like she was a miracle fallen from the sky.

7

Ty knew he wasn't being smooth, but he couldn't seem to do much about it.

Mallory wasn't just beautiful—which she absolutely was—she was also a smokejumper. That was about the coolest thing he could imagine.

He made sure that she was set up in a lawn chair under one of the few shade maples. It was in the grassy area along the edge of their paved corner of the Missoula airport. It was close by the Zulies' white-and-brown headquarters building. The Missoula smokejumpers were fully engaged in this firefight, and all of their tanker assets were as well. There was a hustle and buzz of activity all around them that resounded with activity. Air tankers ripped down out of the sky. In minutes, they were loaded up with a thousand gallons or more of viscous red fire retardant and sent back aloft. It was a bad fire and more assets were streaming in every minute. He recognized outfits from Boise and Utah. No one else from Washington or Oregon yet, but they were facing big fires of their own.

Ty did what he could to make sure Mallory stuck around as long as possible. Not that there was much he could do, other than make her comfortable. He did place a water bottle close by her good hand after cracking the lid for her. He set a reminder on his phone for two hours so that he could make sure she iced her wrist on schedule and another for three hours when she could take more painkillers.

It was so hard not to stare at her.

Not just the long blonde hair the color of the sun—even nicer than Jana's which was saying something. Or the sky blue eyes. Not even the incredible physique that had been revealed when the nurse had stripped off her Nomex fire shirt and revealed the form-fitting black t-shirt beneath. It was the t-shirt itself that had really gotten him.

*This is what AWESOME smokejumpers look like.*

Big yellow letters declared it without question. He'd never been that confident about anything in his life. And there Mallory sat, so sure of herself. So perfect.

He jolted to his feet as a flight of the Firebirds came in for service. Amos, Curt, and Jasper on the first flight. Near enough noon. While the trio of helos were refueled and the pilots stretched out the kinks, he scrabbled together food bags for them and cold sodas. They'd already been aloft for four hours while he'd been at the hospital, making this their second refueling stop. Maggie changed air filters without even checking them first. They'd blow them clean and reinsert them on the next service if they were still good. He scrubbed bugs and soot off the windscreens.

In moments they were aloft and the next flight was inbound: Stacy, Palo, and Drew.

"Holy shit!" Drew whispered when he spotted Mallory under the tree.

Ty didn't hesitate. He slammed a water bottle into one of Drew's hands, and then an elbow into his gut.

"Whoa! Sorry man," Drew laughed. "Didn't know you'd already staked the territory."

"I didn't!" How could he? He just didn't like someone else talking about Mallory with that tone. Not even Drew—who he knew was a total dog when it came to women. His and Amos' reputations were notorious on and off the fireline.

"Uh-oh. Somebody's got it bad," Drew's laugh followed him.

He checked in with Palo who didn't offer Mallory more than a glance. "Who's she?"

"She's the smokejumper. Busted-up wrist."

Palo just nodded, then snagged an arm around Maggie's waist as she hurried by. He slammed her into a hug and kiss, then let her go about her work without a single word. But they were both smiling.

Ty couldn't help glancing sideways at Mallory, but she was talking with Stacy.

8

"Thanks for saving me."

"Glad we made it in time. Thanks for being quick to dump your chute when the tree broke. That chunk of tree probably weighed more than my helo. Would have been bad."

Mallory smiled up at Stacy. But she couldn't help notice Ty watching her from under the flop of his hair.

"What's his story?" Then she kinda wished she hadn't asked.

Stacy didn't glance around, but did give her a knowing smile—just the way Meaghan used to when a boy was hitting on Mallory. "Ty has been our handyman all summer. He's good. We're really going to miss him when he goes back to school."

Mallory watched him as he hustled among the three helos. He moved like he knew what he was doing. He also kept doing extra things. Because Stacy wasn't in her helo, Mallory could see him double-checking several things he hadn't on the others and dropping a fresh water bottle into a holder.

"Well, gotta fly now," then Stacy winked at her. "Ty's a damn good kid."

Mallory laughed. Stacy couldn't be more than her late twenties, but they were both "kids" to her. Stacy caught the joke, shrugged good naturedly, and hurried back to her helo. In moments, the three of them were aloft.

Ty spent another twenty minutes dealing with various items—clearly preparing for the next round— then slouched into a chair beside her.

"And now we wait." He didn't sound unhappy about it. Just a fact of life.

"It's weird. I've never seen this part of operations."

"That's because you're always out there being amazing." She wished that he'd tell that to her parents. Her brother would have said it, if he'd come back alive from the Iraq War. He'd have been surprised that she'd broken out of the girly-girl mode she'd been in since forever, but he'd have cheered her on. Two years now and her parents were still waiting for her to "come to her senses."

Ty continued, half speaking to himself. "Thought I was doing something. But you make me feel as if I haven't done shit all summer."

"Stacy seemed to think otherwise. They're all awfully nice."

"I guess," Ty slouched lower.

They chatted through the long afternoon—lazy hours in between moments of frenetic activity. Soon there were the four of them under the tree—Jana with the flight operations radio and Maggie updating her maintenance logs—all shifting their chairs along with the sun to stay in the shade. By late afternoon, it wasn't an issue. The valley where Missoula lay between three mountain ranges slowly filled with smoke until it blocked the sun, erasing shadows. Soon they were donning dust masks.

It took her a while to get comfortable around Jana. That missing hand bothered her more than she wanted to show.

Maggie, who'd just finished another refueling, plummeted into a chair as if exhausted beyond ever moving again.

Mallory had learned through the day that the Firebirds' head mechanic never sat still for long. When she wasn't rushing around a helo, or preparing to, she fussed with the three pickups. No wonder they all looked so perfect. She had a bubbly energy that never let go.

"You two could be sisters," Maggie knocked back half a Coke, as if she needed more caffeine to supercharge her effervescence.

Mallory felt herself turning to face Jana. How close had she come to losing her hand? Then they'd have *really* matched.

"Maybe not sisters, but like really close cousins or something."

Jana, who Mallory had learned didn't speak much, raised her hooks in wry acknowledgement.

Maggie didn't miss the gesture. "Okay. Crappy analogy, but you're both gorgeous blondes. Jana," Maggie leaned forward in a conspiratorial whisper, "swept the feet out from under the ever-so-cute Jasper when she was just ten—even if it took them until last month to figure that out. And now you've knocked our Ty for a total loop. Don't you just love men?" Then she bounced to her feet and was on the move again.

Mallory didn't want to turn to Ty, but couldn't stop herself.

He was frozen as solid as the ice pack he'd fished out of the cooler and was wrapping in a towel to drape over her arm. He'd been so solicitous all afternoon: remembering when her painkillers were wearing off, making sure she ate and stayed hydrated. He'd even arranged a radio relay though Stacy so that she could check in with Krista and let her jump leader know where she'd ended up—he'd already gotten the message about her wrist relayed while they were still in the hospital.

Through the day, Mallory had come to simply accept Ty's kindness. But Maggie was right, it was more than that. And he wasn't doing the testosterone-poisoned thing either. He was simply taking care of her.

And now he was glowing brighter red than any forest fire.

"Ty?"

"Uh-huh."

"Aren't your hands getting cold?" They were still wrapped around the ice pack.

"Uh-huh." Still he didn't move.

She didn't "just love men" the way Maggie had said it. With her unstoppable effusive energy, and her majorly cute Latina looks, it was easy to bet that men loved her as well.

But Ty was being beyond kind and beyond cute.

Mallory extracted the ice pack from his hands, and laid it over her wrist. After the initial shock, the cold felt good, soothing.

Then she leaned in and brushed her lips over his.

He remained frozen in place, his eyes shooting wide.

Then, just before she was going to pull away, he sighed softly and leaned into the kiss.

# 9

Ty could feel the shock of the kiss all the way down to his toes. He'd had full-on wild sex that didn't live up to the wonder of Mallory's kiss.

He was supposed to be the worldly one: twenty-one, college-educated (at least partly—not sure why though), and…and…something.

Mallory was just twenty, straight from high school into the smokejumpers, doing her forest ecology coursework mostly online.

Yet he was the one humbled by the fact that she'd kissed him. Humbled and—*Holy Crap, Batman*—majorly turned on. She had a kiss that didn't allow him to do anything but feel and give back the best he could. It was the kind of kiss that didn't allow any chance she was playing a head game—like kissing him at a frat party to upset some boyfriend, or seeking revenge sex, or…

Mallory simply kissed him. And when she was done and moved back, his ears buzzed louder than a flight of incoming helos.

No…exactly that loud.

Jana snapped her hooks together about a half inch off the tip of his nose.

He blinked at her, then at the three helos settling close beside them.

"Yipes!" He pushed out of the chair, but something was wonky with his balance. He shook his head to clear it and got on the move.

Behind him he heard Mallory's delighted laugh, and his equilibrium went haywire again.

## 10

*B*ecause she was bored to death, the Firebirds let her help on Day Two. Nothing fancy, handing out water bottles, whatever. Better than sitting still.

Day Three they stopped treating her like some fragile guest and treated her the same way they would anyone else on the team who had a bunged-up wrist.

Krista and the rest of the Hoodies were pulled out on Day Four for a break. The fire was still running ugly, only ten percent contained, but that ten percent had been where the Hoodies had fought it to a standstill. Four days in had earned them twelve hours sack time before they'd be jumping back into a new sector.

Mallory had helped where she could to make sure that the gear was all squared away for the next jump.

"You doing okay, Mal?" Krista was the only one other than her dead brother who got to call her that. Even if becoming a smokie had started as a way to honor his memory, it had now become her lifeblood.

They were sitting on the jump deck of a Sherpa C-23 jump plane with their feet dangling just over the airport's tarmac as the sun finished setting. The smoke layer shifted from blood red toward true darkness.

"I am." And she was, much to her own surprise. "I mean I'd rather be jumping but," she raised her arm in its sling and shrugged.

"That's good. You handled that great by the way. Kept your head all the way through. Knew you were something special since that first day."

Mallory bumped shoulders with Krista. Krista was built on a massive scale—at least three Mallorys packed into her powerful frame. She was the big sister Mallory never had and the beloved brother who she'd lost rolled into one.

"Something else on your mind." Krista never missed a thing.

Half a thousand, but Mallory chickened out with the one she already knew the answer to. "Next season?"

"Will take care of next season. You heal up, do whatever the doc says, we'll be jumping together again soon enough."

Mallory planted a kiss on Krista's shoulder. *Best big sister in the world.*

"What's his name?" She didn't miss that either.

"Ty," she sighed. Apparently it was time to jump to the real question.

"Hump him blind yet?"

"Krista!"

"Guess not. Why not?"

"He's just…" she didn't know what. "He's just kind."

"And obviously kisses good enough that you want to hump him blind."

"Krista!"

"Just sayin'. You know how I'm plainspoken and all." And it wasn't an affectation. Her husband and fellow smokie, Evan, often described her as "subtle as an uncontained wildfire"—which was true.

"You never were one to mess around." Krista had never pulled a verbal punch in her life. Probably not a real one either.

"Not once I found Evan."

"And did you hump *him* blind?" Mallory couldn't believe she'd asked the question. Or was even having this conversation.

"Damn straight! About two minutes after your high school's smokejumpers camp with us. You girls left and I dragged him straight off into the woods. We had our way with each other among the ferns. Big time!"

Mallory couldn't help giggling along with Krista's big-throated laugh.

"Gods, I was such a mess at that camp."

"You had it together by the time you left though. Look at yourself, Mal. Look at what you made of yourself. A goddamn smokejumper. Your parents will get that someday, or they won't. Doesn't matter as long as *you* know it. We're tough as Special Forces, Evan always said. He was Green Beret, so I'm gonna trust him on that."

"You just trust him because he married you."

"Yeah," Krista sighed happily. And Krista's bright smile caught the distant airport lights, "He's survived me, too."

"So far," Mallory noted.

"Gives me an idea or two. Wonder if he's still

awake." Krista hopped down and patted Mallory's knee before she strode away.

Mallory didn't want to hump Ty blind…except maybe a little. In the evenings, after sunset chased the helicopters from the sky, the Firebirds would all sit around a small firepit, cooking burgers over the flames and telling stories. Ty had managed to hover and take care of her without making it feel like she was any trouble at all.

She could practically hear Krista's words in Ty's mouth, *A goddamn smokejumper.* She'd impressed the hell out of him. She liked that. A lot. In the past, it had always been her beauty doing the impressing of boys. Ty saw more than that.

After the second night they'd taken a long walk around the airport perimeter, watching the jets from the commercial side of the airport slide in and out through the smoke. Last night, they'd done more than linger along the back fence. They'd done almost everything that could be done while still wearing clothes.

Ty's attraction to her was so big that it seemed to shadow out her past.

When she'd stopped focusing on being the high school's beauty queen, most of her friends had drifted away. As she'd plunged into the academics of botany her senior year, and joined track-and-field to start conditioning her body for the next year's smokejumper tryouts, the boys she used to hang with had drifted away —puzzled by who she'd become. Only her girlfriends in the Outdoors Club, who'd also been at the three-day smokejumpers camp, had understood. Even if they hadn't been prepared for her transformation.

Ty was the first boy who had seen the new her…and couldn't get enough of it.

She could feel him. Out there in the dark even now, waiting for her. Could feel herself wanting to go to him.

11

"Never," was all Ty could manage.

"Never what?" Mallory's voice was barely a breath as she lay beneath him on the blanket. He'd carried it out here, along with a pocketful of foiled-wrapped hope, just on the off chance that she'd come find him and want…

He sighed again, unable to do more. He'd imagined sex with Mallory, but he'd never imagined this.

There was no privacy, no space at the Zulies' base. Especially not with all of the other outfits on site. There were smokies and pilots in every bunk. Hotshots crashed out on the floor and camped on the grass out by the US Forest Service building. Anything as gentle as commercial Boeing 737s roaring along the runway couldn't wake a firefighter fresh off a big burn.

Instead, Mallory had come to him in the place they'd found last night. It was a small wood beyond the north end of the runway, just inside the perimeter fence. Each jet's landing lights flickered through the trees, dappling her perfect body with light flashing faster than a high school gym disco ball. The power of the jets passing less than a hundred feet overhead was nothing compared to the power of what had just passed between them.

When she'd peaked just as a jet had flashed overhead, she'd let loose a laughing scream that overflowed with joy. He'd joined his shout to hers and it had been like nothing before in his life.

"Never what?"

"I'm a guy. I can't speak right now."

"Uh-huh," Mallory kept one arm and both her legs wrapped firmly about him. She snuggled in tighter.

"Never felt anything even close to that. It wasn't just sex. It was... I dunno. Something incredible. You're amazing, Mallory."

"I am. So are you, Ty."

"I wish."

"Hey! How can you not think you're amazing after that? We did really, really good."

Ty hid his face in her hair. Yeah, it was dumb. It was their first time together. But he knew he'd never get tired of Mallory. Not for a minute, not for a second. The smell of her. The taste. The joy that radiated from every move, every look.

It was fine for Ty Franks. He could deserve it. Except he didn't really, because "Ty Franks" didn't exist.

Ty buried his face even deeper in Mallory's glorious hair and wished like hell that he was actually himself and not someone else.

## 12

After ten long days, the fire was drawing to a close. And so was his summer.

None of that mattered anymore.

What mattered was Mallory. They hadn't gone to their wood beneath the jets every night—though each time they did it was even more memorable than the first. But even the nights they'd just lain together in their bags among the sleeping helo pilots curled up on the grass were remarkable.

It was as if the amazing sex was no longer the only thing that mattered. In the past, that had always been the defining and sometimes sole purpose of his relationships. With Mallory it was only one part of an amazing amount of greatness.

She'd unfolded her past like a book. Each page so clear. How the death of her big brother had almost destroyed her until she'd found smokejumping. She understood what parts of herself were broken and had fixed them. She talked about the parts she still didn't understand but was working on. All the time with her head on his shoulder and her injured arm resting negligently on his chest as if they belonged together. As if there was such a thing as being happy together for more than a couple nights.

The passage of time had been marked by little of note. They'd gone back to the hospital for new x-rays and to replace the splint with a cast. The days themselves had been punctuated by good days of hard work. The nights by startling sex and intimate conversation. Or maybe by intimate sex and startling conversation.

He'd told her about his mom, some. Made it clear how much it hurt when she'd died last year so that she'd leave the subject alone. He never mentioned his bastard of a father. Friends growing up. College—leaving after the second week of his junior year to take care of Mom. Those had been safe topics. But he couldn't tell her about anything that really mattered like—

"You're confusing the crap out of me, Mallory." He hadn't really intended to say that to her, but they'd both gotten into the habit of just speaking their thoughts to each other.

"In a good way, I hope," her voice was sleepy and just a little teasing as it often was after what they now called jet-sex.

The wind had shifted three days ago, driving the fire right into the massively prepared firebreaks, and it was dying fast.

It had also flipped the direction of the flight pattern into the airport, because planes always took off and landed into the wind.

Now, instead of idling jets easing down close overhead as if held up by the pillars of their landing lights illuminating columns in the smoke, they roared aloft—heavily laden and under full throttle. The bright landing lights were replaced by little flashes of red and green from the wingtips. And the engines' big-throated howl echoed through their joined bodies as they rode out the jet's passage so close above them. They'd taken to keeping an ear out for jets leaving the terminal and taxiing to the far end of the runway. Getting a good head start on jet-sex had interrupted any number of conversations.

But now when he needed the interruption…

It was late and flights were few and far between.

"Ty?" Mallory murmured into his shoulder.

Her hair lay over his neck and shoulders like a silk blanket. He could lose himself in gliding his hands over the surprising muscles in her sleek frame. From shoulders down to—

"Ty!" She propped herself up with forearm and cast on his chest. The edges of it itched.

"My name isn't Ty."

Mallory jolted as if he'd slapped her.

He lifted his head up to look at her in the soft spill of the airport's lights reflected off the smoky sky. Then, giving up, he thudded the back of his head down on the blanket he'd spread beneath them. He did it again, harder, but it didn't help.

## 13

Mallory didn't know how to react. A lie? She sworn off those ever since she'd recognized the lie that she was okay with her brother's death. It was only then that she was able to forgive him for dying somewhere so far away. Lies were something high school boys did to get you alone in a dark corner. She knew all about those lies.

But Ty hadn't been like that—except now he said he wasn't Ty. Maybe he was like that. But then why would he confess. He wasn't the only one confused here.

"Who are you?"

"Fuck if I know." He pounded his head back on the ground once more.

"Cut that out!"

He sighed miserably, but stopped.

"Anything else you've been lying about other than your name?" Like how miraculous and important he'd made her feel? Had that been a lie too? She didn't know if she could stand it if it had been.

He tipped his head to one side then the other, before sighing again.

"Not to you. At least not that I can think of."

Mallory sat up, wincing as she forgot to not use her injured hand. She pulled on her shirt, finding it awkward without Ty's help. How many ways had she come to depend on him? But she'd depended on who she *thought* he was. If he was really something else…

"What's your name?"

"Barlow. Barlow Williams."

"I think I like Ty better."

"Barlow Williams the Second. My dad was the First."

She knew who Ty Franks was. Barlow Williams II? Not so much.

"Tyrone was my mom's dad. Franks was her last name."

"So, you *are* Ty, sort of." She knew she was grasping at straws, but she'd come to rely on him far more than made sense. It was as if he was the only one who saw her. Little sister to smokies. "Besieged by some madness," according to her parents' exact words. Ty saw both *her* and the smokejumper. At times it was hard to tell which he was more attracted to and she'd liked that feeling—liked it a lot!

He shrugged a yes then flopped an arm over his eyes.

"Why the lie?" Mallory resisted the urge to just run away.

"God I hate that word. Makes me sound like a total weasel." He didn't look out from under his arm.

"So, stop weaseling and answer the question."

With each second that he lay there in silence,

Mallory could feel herself growing colder despite the warm evening.

"I can't."

Mallory rocked back. She'd shared so much with him. Had been fearing the end of the summer, of this fire. She'd never given herself to someone so completely—never! The sex, the holding, the caring—they had become a little bubble of cosmic perfection until the moment Tyrone-Barlow-whoever-the-hell-he-was had busted it all apart.

She scrabbled around in the dark for her pants and boots. To hell with her underwear, wherever it had gone.

"Mallory?"

No way she was going to answer him.

"Can you help me?"

"Help you?" She spoke despite herself. "Think up another fake name so you can lie to me some more?"

"No," his voice sounded so sad that she stopped with one boot on and one boot off. He'd even tied her bootlaces for her. She stuffed the laces into her boot top rather than try to figure it out in the dark.

"Then what?"

"I have to tell Curt and Jana the truth. But I don't know how to do it."

"The truth is easy. You just say it." Which wasn't the truth at all. Her parents kept pushing her away because of her own truth. "Okay. That's wrong. It can be hard as hell, but you say it anyway."

Ty lay still. He didn't argue, and she didn't quite have the heart to leave him there.

# 14

Ty tried to get Jana and Curt off alone. But it didn't work.

The Firebirds had been released overnight. It was just past dawn and they were loading up the helos on the trailers, doublechecking that they had all their gear, and saying their goodbyes. Two other outfits were released as well—the rest were still in full firefight hustle. The wide pavement in front of the Zulies' headquarters were a mass of people and machinery.

He and Mallory had spread out their sleeping bags separately. Not far apart, but apart. And he'd missed her every minute of the sleepless night as he'd watched the slowly turning stars.

But he finally got Jana and Curt aside, sitting on one of the lowboy trailers while he stood awkwardly in front of them not knowing where to begin.

Before he could, Jasper and Stacy naturally gravitated over and sat with their partners.

And wherever the other two women went, Maggie joined. Of course she was holding hands with Palo.

Then it was clear that Drew and Amos didn't want to be left out of whatever was happening. Soon they were all crowded around, some on the edge of the lowboy, others in lawn chairs. Someone gave him one and he dropped into it. Mallory slipped elegantly into the one beside him—after moving it a slight distance away.

The truth, in his opinion, totally sucked.

He thought he'd blown it totally with Mallory last night, but she was still here. Maybe there was a sliver of hope. It was all he had, so he'd use that.

"I'm done for the season."

No surprise there. The long fire had burned to within two days of his already announced departure date.

"Missoula's my home town. I grew up here. I go—" another piece of the lie. "I went to college here."

Only Mallory glanced at him at that admission.

"I…" It caught in his throat.

The truth *was* hard to say.

"I'm not—" He balled his fists to fight the tears as his throat choked off.

"He's not Ty Franks," Mallory said for him softly. He didn't know whether to be angry for her unfairly taking the load that was his shit or hug her in thanks. Except he'd given up that privilege—all because of the goddamn lie in the first place. But still, she'd helped cover for him, just as he'd helped when Mallory had fixated on Jana's hooks after the hospital.

The head of the New Mexico hotshot team came over to say goodbye before they loaded up for the long drive to a Santa Rosa fire in Northern Cal.

Once he left, Ty forced himself to look around the

circle of these people he'd come to know so well over the summer.

Mostly puzzled. Pissed would come soon enough.

Except Jana. She was smiling at him. Except Jana never smiled.

"I was wondering how long you were going to sit on that," her smile didn't abate.

He opened his mouth, but no sound came out.

"I pay you every two weeks, Ty. I also report it to the government. They contacted me about a name discrepancy for the Social Security number that you gave me."

"A…"

"What's going on?" Curt turned to his sister.

"Ty's real name is Barlow Williams." Now Jana was the one speaking for him.

"That's weird. Same as Dad?"

"The Second," Jana finished.

"That really weird," Curt continued to look confused.

Stacy held Curt's hand more tightly and blinked in surprise a couple of times then gave a puzzled laugh, "I have a brother-in-law?"

"You have a what?" Curt looked at his wife.

"Half-brother-in-law," Jana corrected.

Ty was trying desperately to get a handle on what was happening. They were supposed to be angry or… or something! He turned to Mallory, but she was keeping her lovely face carefully blank.

"So he's…" Curt stopped himself. "So we're…" he waved a finger back and forth between his own chest and Ty's. "That's beyond really weird."

"Weird wasn't my word for it," Ty was surprised he could speak.

"Pissed as hell," Jasper said quietly from under the brim of his cowboy hat. "How did you find out?"

"I found your dad's, *our* dad's name on the marriage license while going through Mom's shit after she died last year. I searched online and you guys popped up. She told me my dad had died when I was a little boy. In a car accident. Even though I found notes of meetings in hotels, and a vacation together when I was fifteen. I don't think I ever met him. Not once."

"Marriage license? Dad married both your mom *and* ours?" Curt shook his head but couldn't seem to clear it. "What's worse than beyond weird?"

"Mega-weird?" Mallory suggested and Curt nodded his agreement.

"Car wreck came true twenty years later," Jana stayed her usual totally chill, rational self. "I wonder if he lived long enough after the accident to see the irony."

Then she looked right at him.

"Our mom was pretty good. Dad was always a self-centered prick."

"Hey!" Curt protested.

"He was, Curt," Jana said with a sigh before turning back to Ty. "Your half-brother always thinks the best of people. Kind of a blind spot."

Ty knew that. Couldn't miss it because that *was* the kind of guy Curt was. None of this was going the way he expected. He glanced over at Mallory who was watching him carefully.

*Truth is as hard as hell, but you say it anyway.*

He knew that if he wanted even a half chance with her, he'd have to come clean, all the way.

She nodded once, as if she could read what he was thinking.

He reached out his hand and, after a moment's hesitation, she took it. It was the strongest he ever felt. He turned back to his unknown family, knowing what he had to do.

"I'm broke. I can't pay for college. Mom died busted too. Jasper's right, I was so furious when I found out you two had your pretty little Firebirds. I—" This was worse than hard.

Mallory squeezed his hand, so he closed his eyes and blurted it out.

"I came here to screw you guys. Gather information, get some dirt on you. Sue you for half of the money. He was my dad, too." Despite the bigamy and lies and never wanting to see him and— Remembering his mom's strength at the end was all that let him keep it together.

"Does it make you feel any better to know that after we sold the house and everything else, we ended up *owing* over twenty thousand dollars?"

"Why was that anyway?" Curt asked.

"You remember how money slid through his fingers. Cars, the boat. The helicopter lessons that he paid for without even blinking… All of it. Remember how many times he changed jobs yet we were always broke? The fights he and Mom always had about money?" Jana waved her hooks in the air like she was brushing it away.

Curt grunted as she jogged his memory.

Ty had always thought they were so lucky because they got to have their father and he didn't. But Ty and his mom had never fought. Money had been tight, but they'd both been careful and worked hard. She insisted that college was his way out, but that hadn't come together and he hadn't had the heart to tell her about what a waste it all was—even with in-state tuition and scholarships covering most of it.

He and Mom had been a team. Them against the world. It sounds like Barlow the First maybe hadn't been such a great gift after all.

But Ty couldn't help looking at the six glistening helicopters perched on their trailers behind the three black pickups. He'd looked it up and the six helos cost over ten million dollars.

"Army disability pay. Gave me a medal and bump in rank on my way out the door for this," Jana held up her prosthetic hand. "Also every penny Curt and Jasper had set aside in six years of flying to fire. We started the season hocked out to everybody. We've paid off the trucks and one of the helicopters, better than I thought. Might own a second by end of season. The rest are a lease and a prayer."

Ty started to laugh. He couldn't help it.

Jana waited him out. Somehow his half-sister was the only one to get the joke. No, Mallory's smile said that she did too.

"Well, that was another one of my famous plans gone bust."

The others started laughing too, but Jana stayed serious until the others quieted.

She leaned in and really looked him in the eye.

"The Ty that first showed up to join us, I'm guessing that's not the kind of person your mother raised."

And with those simple words, Ty felt more like crying than laughing.

"You've been with us all summer. You've done a great job. So, I'm going to make you an offer."

He could only blink in surprise.

"You've mentioned college only three times all summer. I'm guessing it doesn't have you hooked."

Ty looked up at her, "Kind of obvious, huh?"

"Been watching you with Maggie. She says you've got good instincts about aircraft."

"You've talked about me…" He shut his mouth.

"How about the Firebirds fund you for an airframe-and-powerplant course. To pay it off, you come back as assistant mechanic next spring?"

"You'd do that?" Ty tried to gauge his own reaction, but couldn't get a handle on it. It was too big to make sense of all at once.

Jana nodded.

"Why?" Still unable to measure it, he thought how it had felt to help rebuild those engines. It had been fascinating how they actually worked. He could still see it in his head.

"It's not because we're related to the same selfish prick. It's because you're good people. You spent a whole summer proving that despite yourself, Ty. Think about that. You might also want to think about changing at least your first name. Ty fits you way better than some jerk named Barlow. And if I needed more proof that you're good people…" she nodded at Mallory.

It was hard, but Ty made himself look over at her. What was her reaction to all this?

Somehow, impossibly, Mallory looked at him like she believed in him.

"But…" —if he was with the Firebirds and she was a smokie for Mount Hood, they'd never be together.

And that suddenly struck him as the very worst thing that could ever happen.

"One more season with us. I called Denise with MHA. She said she'd look you over after a second season under Maggie's thumb. If you're as good as Maggie and I think you can be, you could go wrench for Mallory's outfit. By the way, there's a top A&P mechanic's course about ten miles from where Mallory and her busted wrist will be stuck in a classroom all winter studying forestry."

Jana rose to her feet and Ty could only stumble to his. Because Mallory hadn't let go of his hand, she rose with him—and took a half step closer.

"We're going down to the passenger terminal and get a decent breakfast before we hit the road. If you two decide you want a lift back to Portland, we could probably make some space."

And the Firebirds all headed after Jana.

Maggie gave him a thumbs up. Stacy left behind a quick hug. Amos and Drew stopped just long enough to tell Mallory that she was too pretty for him and should consider a real man.

Curt shook his hand, strong and solid. "Still say it's beyond mega-weird."

Jasper just nodded from beneath his cowboy hat the way he always did.

Then there was just the two of them standing beside the big pickups. With his free hand, he reached out to stroke his fingers over one of the MD 520Ns. They were so beautiful. Brilliant machines that did a tough job in a very special way.

Even though he could feel her hand still in his, it was difficult to turn and look at Mallory. When he finally did, the sun caught her hair and blazed brilliantly.

"Mallory?" Ty didn't know what the question was, and by her bright blush, neither did she.

"You—" she gasped a little, then caught her breath. He saw the smokejumper come over her as she stood straighter and looked him square in the eye. "You did that great. And you see the real me. Do you have any idea what a gift that is?"

"Yeah. No one sees me." He'd spent a whole life being an outsider to everyone except his mom.

Mallory took that final half step to him and rested a hand on his cheek, "I do."

"And you want to be around me, despite that?"

She didn't answer him with a smile, she used a kiss instead.

He wrapped his arms around her and buried his face in her glorious hair. He'd been keeping his distance for far too long.

There was a new truth and they both held it close because it was the best thing they'd ever do.

# TWICE THE HEAT

*Drew Shaw* and *Amos Berkowitz* *could be twins. They laugh like twins, they tease each other like twins, and they're both wildland firefighting helicopter pilots from the Big Apple and proud of it.*

*Except Drew hails from New York's Upper West Side, while Amos prides himself on his Brooklyn heritage.*

*Julie* and *Natalie Falcone* *are twins. And after a season fighting fires as Hotshots the last thing they want to tangle with are the likes of Drew and Amos. But one fire leads to another and then the heat really starts to build.*

*Enjoy this heartwarming conclusion to the Oregon Firebirds short story series.*

# INTRODUCTION

The conclusion to this series is a story of two guys. I've written some really fun guy-guy buddy teams over the years. Tim and Big John throughout the Night Stalkers series. Chad and Duane romp in Delta Force. And even Mark Henderson and Michael Gibson in the short story *Heart of the Storm* (Night Stalkers short stories #3).

Amos and Drew come from two very different corners of New York City. New York figured prominently in my youth (which is why it appears in so many of my stories). My grandmother lived on the Upper West Side. I also used to ride the train down from Poughkeepsie to catch a Broadway show. When I had a darkroom, I went to the now faded away Photo District to outfit it (and also eat the best pizza in the world out of a little hole-in-the-wall right in the heart of the district). My sister introduced me to the lower East Side and Brooklyn.

So setting up two guys from the city who might as well be twins, but weren't, was a hoot. But this wasn't a buddy tale, it was a buddy-tale-in-which-they-find-true-love story.

Who better to take on the challenge of two guys who act like twins than *actual* twins. Which set two real challenges for me as a writer.

One was how to have the twins-of-spirit and the twins-of-blood behave differently. Real-life twins, in my experience, talk far less than others—because they don't need to in order to communicate. Partial sentences and finishing them for others is standard practice. I knew one set of twins back in high school well enough that I could at least partially follow their twin code, but it was tricky.

Whereas the guys who aren't actually twins? For them it is, perhaps unconsciously, all about the show of *proving* they're that close and understand each other that well. So, I had fun with the two twin sets' speech.

The catch with having twin romances, especially in a short story, was how to create two love stories in a space that normally would barely fit one. You'll see my final solution, but know that it was far from my first attempt to solve that particular puzzle.

1

"Going in."

"On your tail, bro," Amos followed close behind Drew's helicopter. "We're like stooping pigeons nailing those breadcrumbs."

"That's 'stooping hawks,' you dweeb. And those are fifteen hundred degree breadcrumbs." Drew carved an arc and dumped his load of water from the MD 520N's belly tank. Two hundred gallons sheeted down the front of the already burning house.

"But we're super brave pigeons." With most of the burning cedar doused for the moment—what doofus shingled with cedar and didn't keep the forest cut back from his house—Amos decided to dump his own fifteen hundred pounds of water across the burning trees that had ignited the front of the house in the first place.

"I'm a brave hawk anyway," Drew Shaw offered up one of his laughs on their private helo-to-helo frequency. "You, Berkowitz, just can't help following me along wherever I go, like the sad Brooklyn pigeon you are."

Now that was playing dirty. "Just making way for your monster Upper West Side ego, bro."

"Yes, some of us are just superior and know it."

Amos considered a couple of different response ploys, but none of them were going to pan out well. Drew was hard to knock down because he was a dashingly handsome black guy with a big smile and a clean-shaved scalp that shone in the sunlight or in the bars. Maybe he waxed it at night. Amos was always the frumpy Jewish sidekick with too much dark curly hair.

So, he let Drew have the round and focused on his flying.

Thankfully this house and the next had big swimming pools. Amos slid over his chosen pool and lowered the snorkel hose from his hovering helo. He hit the pump switch and sighted along the house's second-story deck to hold his altitude while he loaded up. His helo could suck up its own weight in water in under twenty seconds.

"Sure I follow you, Drew. Someone's got to clean up your poo." The FCC got pissy if you said "shit" over the radio—or even "pissy" for that matter. Really cramped a guy's style. What heli-aviation firefighter said "poo"?

It made the rebuttal doubly weak—both late and lame. Drew didn't even deign to answer. Instead, he just flashed one of those lady-killing smiles at him from where he hovered above the next pool over.

Twenty seconds later, Amos killed the pump switch, and lifted high enough to clear the house and return to its front yard. Sometimes they had to fly five or even ten minutes to find a water source. With those constrictions, the little MD 520Ns were of little use. Luckily this part of the wildfire was moving into a well-pooled neighborhood—bad for the neighborhood, but good for them. Saving houses was what the little helos of the Oregon Firebirds did best.

All six were aloft today, but the wildfire's front was such a mess that they'd split into three teams of two instead of their more typical two-of-three arrangement. These houses were on large plots of one and two acres, most with little attention to the wildland-urban interface they were creating. That meant that when a wildfire lit up the forest, it had a tendency to light up the houses as well.

The shared command frequency was quiet. After a long summer and most of fall, the Firebirds all knew their task sequence like it had been hardwired into their nervous system. Tank up. Douse each structure (burning or not) to soak it down. Don't fight the fire to a standstill —wasn't going to happen anyway at two hundred gallons at a time. Instead, cut a wedge and chase the fire around either side of the structure. Residents might not have to mow the lawn for a while, but they'd have a home to come back to.

As the day dragged on, their banter dragged as well. Which was fine. No point in using it all up before they hit the bar after the no-flying-past-sunset rule knocked them out of the sky. The boss had them on a two-beer limit—which was hard to hit because they also had an eight-hour, from-bottle-to-throttle limit and sunrise still came early. But banter and "I fly a firefighting helo for a living"—especially the latter—went a long way to loosening up the ladies for a night or three.

That he'd picked up Dad's workout habits didn't hurt either. Dad had learned the hard way that you couldn't support a family playing Division II soccer in the US. So he'd gotten into fashion photography, but never stopped with the workouts. They'd sweat together most nights in the basement gym. Mom had given up on him and left long before he became successful at fashion. He was successful in more ways then one. Drew had become used to finding hot women, models, randomly being there for breakfast, often wearing little more than one of Dad's shirts. Women liked a ripped guy. Something Amos had proved to himself well enough in high school.

That's how he'd gotten to know Drew—two New York boys both starting Army boot camp at the top of the fitness roster.

## 2

*J*ulie's silence was deeper than usual and it spoke volumes.

"Yeah," Natalie followed the direction of her twin's gaze.

No question, the Falcone sisters were in it deep this time. They'd been sent out to scout this front of the fire for their interagency hotshot crew. The fire northeast of Placerville, California was a late season burn and likely to be one of the last fires of the year, but that didn't make it any less ugly.

"Maybe…" Natalie nodded to the northern ridge.

The southern one had caught due to a wind shift not long after they'd crossed it—cutting them off from the rest of the crew. The main bulk of the fire was descending the rugged slopes from the east and would be here far too soon.

"Not so much," she answered her own thought. Even at a dead run, they'd be hard pushed to get clear over the north ridge before it too caught fire.

"Ouch," Julie could see the gathering smoke there as well as she could.

"Out of the fire…"

"…into the fire."

They both turned west and stared. That was one of the problems with working with your twin, Julie saw the situation as clearly as Natalie herself did. The escarpment to the west was scalable, but it would take time. Dressed in double-layered Nomex and carrying twenty-five pounds of additional gear—not counting their fire axes, the chain saw, or the can of gas—meant it would take too long. Even shedding their gear might not be enough. And if they didn't clear it, the gear they were carrying was their only hope of survival.

Natalie pulled out her radio. "Hotshot patrol to Hotshot command. We're boxed in by fire in Grid 39-04, repeat three-niner-oh-four. Unless the winds change in the next ten minutes, we're going to have to shelter in place."

"Roger that. Julie, Natalie, you start prepping, I'll see if I can get some help."

She shared a look aloft with her sister.

"Smoke ceiling at three hundred and falling," she reported. "We're digging in."

There was a long pause before the acknowledgement came back. Three hundred feet was below where they could safely fly in a couple tankers of flame retardant. "Falling" meant that even the big helos would be shut out from entering this valley far too soon.

"Shelter in place" was the worst option there was on a wildfire. Actually second worst. It was one small, but important step up from being burned alive. She'd talked to survivors, and seen the ones who didn't—crisped despite their foil shelters.

They were past the need for words, not that they used them all that much with each other. With others, conversations always felt awkward and clunky by comparison. She and Julie simply knew.

Julie had a short-blade chainsaw and began clearing a circle. They were in a grove of arroyo willow and crackling-dry needlegrass. Better here than the bay laurel growing close downwind. Laurel burned hot—perhaps hot enough to melt a fire shelter.

While Julie wielded the saw, Natalie dug in with her Pulaski wildland axe. Hotshots worked in teams of twenty, forming long lines to quickly scrape an area down to mineral soil, clearing away all of the organics that could burn. She now had maybe ten minutes to do it by herself.

No shortcuts. She swung the adze of the Pulaski deep enough into the dirt to get below the needlegrass' root system and raked up a five inch-by-two foot swath. In the rhythm borne of a season's hard practice, she thought of an oval: keeping the tool in motion, cycling up, forward, down with minimal overlap on the prior cut, and another hard dig. She had an eight-by-two foot swatch cleared in under a minute. Returning the other way, she opened it up to eight-by-four feet. At six feet wide, there would be just enough room for them to lay their shelters side by side. Every two feet past that would be two more feet of safety from the fire. Fire that had leaped five hundred feet in three minutes to trap them here.

She didn't need to look up to know that Julie was dropping every tree that could fall on them so that they landed to the outside, as if the two of them were the center of an explosion. An explosion that hadn't happened yet, but would far too soon.

Natalie resisted looking up for as long as she could tolerate the unknown. When she couldn't stand it any longer, she sliced one more swath to prove she was stronger than the fear. It was a close call. Ten-by-sixteen feet clear of anything that would burn. But to all sides, she'd now mounded up a berm of dead grass and dead, fallen branches.

She looked at the sky first. The ceiling was down to a hundred feet. A tanker airplane needed at least a five hundred-foot ceiling for even marginal safety. No help coming.

Then she looked east. Minutes. At most. The fire was a living beast that had barely slowed as it crawled down the slope. Once it hit the flatland of the valley floor, it was going to race toward them.

"Two more trees," Julie called.

Natalie didn't even bother to respond. She raced around, busting up the berm of flammables though her arms were screaming with the sustained effort.

It didn't take much to stay motivated.

The fire's roar had become a distinct, basso rock-n-roll note.

That must be what the nineteen members of the Granite Mountain Hotshots who had been killed in the Yarnell burnover had heard. Killed—despite doing exactly the same steps she and Julie were doing. Dozens had survived burnovers with only minor scathing, but it was hard not to think about the Granite Mountain team —all killed at once, except for one lone scout who chance had placed in the clear. This time it was the two scouts who were in it.

Julie arrived in time to break the last berm with her and scatter it as far as they could.

Then they went to the middle of the scraped soil and chopped face holes. When the fire rolled over their shelters, the air would become superheated. By digging a foot-deep hole, they'd be able to breathe cooler air at the worst moments of the fire's passage.

"Now!" Julie cried out. She'd left the chainsaw and gas can back in the trees. They didn't need that exploding close beside them. They tossed their Pulaskis aside. If they so much as snagged the foil shelter on the tip of the axe, it would be a death knell.

They shook the thin shelters out carefully, turned so that the fire's wind ballooned them open. Their silvered coating caught the reds and golds of the nearing fire— almost pretty in the smoke-induced dusk.

"Dante would approve," Natalie wished she could erase the image from the sky the moment she said it.

"The seven circles of Hell brought to life," Julie concurred, reinforcing it in their brains.

*Oh well.* Natalie stepped in, placing her feet at one narrow end. She shrugged it up and over her helmet until all that showed was her front from calves to eyes— like the belly of a silver-backed caterpillar.

There was barely time for a last look around.

"Great idea for a change of pace, Julie."

"I've done better, Nat," Julie admitted.

They had been dating twins. The brothers had been handsome, self-assured, good lovers, and bastard cheating shitheads. The BCSs' non-twin brother had also been Julie and Natalie's boss, until the fiery breakup.

*Let's have an adventure!* Julie's suggestion had led them to trying out for and qualifying on a hotshot team. It had been way better than the clerical dead end they'd been stuck in. At least prior to this moment it had been better…still might be.

"See you on the other side. Love."

"Love. No more twins. Right?"

"Deal!" They said together.

And then they lay down side by side, placed their faces in the dug holes, and waited for the fire.

3

*I*t was late afternoon and the sandwich Amos had managed to cram down at noon was long since burned off. His gut was growling as loud as his helo's Rolls Royce turbine engine.

"Gotta get me a dinner bag on the next refuel, even if I have to eat from it like a horse." He told Drew—an idea which didn't sound all bad. Flying this close to fire took intense concentration and burned up the calories. It took both hands to fly an MD 520N to fire. Finding the third hand to hold a sandwich was tough.

They hovered low over a creek they'd found not far from a winery they were trying to save, loading up water as fast as they could.

"I'm thinking something to hold it, like a large wooden clip," Drew radioed back on their frequency. They always jumped a second radio away from the command frequency so that they could coordinate their own flight—which only had the two of them today.

"You got no imagination, bro. It should look like a beautiful woman's hand, right down to the fingernail polish. Just holding it there, waiting for whenever you're ready for another bite." Water tank full, Amos kicked off the pumps and pulled aloft.

"Like there's a woman on the planet that would do that for a guy from Brooklyn." Drew took the lead toward the winery. They'd already saved the house and wine barn, it was the vineyard they were trying to save now.

"Way before an Upper Westie who—"

"This is Jana," the manager and part owner of the Oregon Firebirds cut in on the command frequency. "Report status by the numbers."

In seconds they'd run the list. Curt and Jasper were headed in for a refuel and food break. Stacy and Palo wouldn't be far behind them. He himself and Drew had enough fuel for another hour aloft.

"Drew and Amos. All haste. Two hotshots. Imminent burnover. Grid three-niner."

"Roger," Drew acknowledged for both of them.

Amos spun his helo to face southeast. The change in direction put him in the lead…and he wished it hadn't. Thirty-nine-oh-four was a blanket of smoke with fire on three sides and moving.

"We're in the Army now," Drew muttered.

They'd both flown OH-58D Kiowa scout helicopters in Iraq; not all that different from their present MD 520Ns. The Kiowas specialized in running low, down between the trees. Then, close to enemy lines, they'd pop up until their rotors were just level with the treetops to expose nothing except their mast-mounted sight—a multi-camera array the size of a beach ball that stuck up above the blades. A very low-profile machine. This was definitely going to be a down-in-the-trees mission. Except this time, rather than hiding in them to *avoid* enemy fire, the trees themselves were *on* fire.

He yanked up on the collective with his left hand and shoved the cyclic joystick forward with his right for maximum speed.

Unable to get any height because of the smoke ceiling, he veered left as they entered the grid area. Thirty-nine-oh-four was a kilometer-wide square between the burning hills, most of it covered with moderate-to-dense growth in the twenty- to forty-meter tall range.

About a third of it was already burning—flames leaping skyward, thick smoke in billows that looked like speeded-up film they were moving so fast. Trees literally exploding as their sap was superheated straight into steam.

Somewhere, in all that madness, they were looking for a pair of silver shelters the size of people.

Amos didn't have to look to know Drew would veer right. They'd run up the outside of the square, as close to the encroaching fire as they dared, box across the top, then down the middle before starting a square-pattern search. They'd done the move a hundred times in the Army and didn't need to talk about it.

Jana had given them the hotshot's radio frequency but he was getting no response.

"Got a feeling," he told Drew over the radio.

"Yeah, not a good one either."

Two reasons they wouldn't answer: they were in the fire already, or it was so close to them they couldn't hear the call over the roaring of the flames.

That was it!

"They're somewhere close by the firefront. Can't hear us."

Drew didn't answer. He'd be doing the same things Amos was.

Watching out for low smoke and tall trees.

Searching the terrain below for a flicker of silver foil shelter.

And nursing every single knot of speed he could out of his helicopter.

4

Natalie lay with her face in the dirt.

"Don't come out, even when you think it's safe," she shouted at Julie. Julie already knew that, of course, but this was no time to rely on half-spoken twin-code.

"You don't either," Julie shouted back. Her voice was muffled by the two shelters.

They had their hands raised to either sides of their heads, hooked inside the foil to keep it pinned tight to the ground. The shelters were set close enough that they were in contact from elbow-to-wrist and boot-to-boot… and never had the distance felt greater. Foil shelters, heavy leather gloves, and the chasm of possibly imminent death.

"If you take one, please take both," she whispered to the fire gods. That was why they'd dated twins in the first place. As much as they drove each other crazy on occasion, she never wanted to live further than next door from her sister. Finding a way for men not to come between… *Yeah*, it had led to their current predicament

—no matter how indirectly—but it didn't change the truth.

Something else not to leave to twin code. "I lov—"

The fire's roar, which had been building steadily, suddenly redoubled.

Quadrupled!

In training they'd told them that the fire-driven winds would batter at the shelter and she'd thought she'd be ready for that. Not even close.

The shelter's thin material hammered against her as if driving her into the dirt. It rippled and roared. The flapping was so fierce that it was hard to imagine that the material wouldn't shred, and harder still to keep it pinned to the ground.

Then there came the hammer blow!

So hard it almost hurt. It definitely knocked the wind out of her—and perhaps a scream with it.

Then…water came seeping in under the edge of the foil. In moments she went from lying on dirt to lying in mud. Her facehole filled with water until she had to raise her head to breathe.

"What the—"

"Unshelter now!" The command roared out at her.

She hesitated. It went against all training.

"Now!" It boomed over a PA system close enough to hurt her ears.

She took a deep breath, held it, and peeked. She was looking directly at a large metal bar hovering just inches from her face. Natalie had to blink twice to make sense of it…

It was a helicopter skid hovering inches over an area awash with water.

And close behind it was a tower of flame.

She didn't need to be told a third time. Not bothering to unshelter, she rose, grabbed the door handle and dove into the back of the small helo. She felt it lift, turn, and begin to move.

Only after she was in did her brain kick in.

"Julie!" The scream ripped out of her throat as she tried to wrestle the foil out of her face and see.

"Damn, lady. No need to shout, I can hear you." A man's voice. The pilot's? Didn't matter.

"Julie!" She shouted at him. "My sister!"

"My bro's got her," the pilot replied calmly.

Natalie finally managed to sit up and get the foil out of her face to look out the side window. A second helo flew close beside them. And there, still shrouded in silver, was Julie's face also plastered against the rear window.

She slapped the flat of her hand against the glass—and the door swung part way open.

"Shit!" She yanked it shut and latched it this time.

When Natalie looked out again, Julie waved. That was all that mattered.

"Any last words?" the pilot asked drily.

Natalie wondered what he was talking about. Then she looked between the two pilot seats out the windshield…and wished she hadn't. Apparently there was still more to care about. A lot more.

5

"Well, this looks like fun," Drew transmitted over the radio.

"What we live for," Amos did his best to keep it light.

They'd spotted the shelters in unison, too damn close to the center of the firefront. They probably should have bailed and let the sheltered hotshots take their chances. They'd made themselves a good hide. He and Drew should have dropped their water in a wedge between the fire and the shelters then gotten the hell out.

That was fire safety training.

But that wasn't Army training. "Leave no man behind" wasn't a motto, it was a way of life. The most elite rescue team of them all, the pararescue jumpers had the motto "That others may live." He and Drew had talked plenty about what *that* kind of commitment took. Talked about it enough that it too had become a part of them.

Now it looked as if that motto might come true.

They'd dumped their loads into the fire just above the shelters, then gone in to either side.

Thankfully, the hotshots had loaded fast, but it might not be fast enough. The fire had circled. Both of the side burns were swinging in to close the gap. Any part of the valley not filled with fire was being obscured by smoke.

Going straight up would seem to make sense, but that way lay another kind of hurt. Even if the air controllers cleared the airspace of fast-moving tanker planes, traveling up into the smoke was bad news. It meant their air filters would be eating ash and all of them trying to breathe superheated air. Even filtered, it wasn't something he ever wanted to try.

"Fast and low, buddy," he called out.

"Fast and low," Drew answered back as they slalomed ahead.

Drew had the lead by ten feet, so Amos let him slide ahead. He tucked in one rotor diameter back and five feet up—just high enough that their rotors wouldn't intermesh in the case of a sudden move. Rather than watching ahead, he just watched Drew's helo. They'd perfected this back when dodging anti-aircraft—two helos flying like they were one.

Each tiny control maneuver that the lead pilot made, the tail pilot did the same. While the follow-position took immense concentration, it was concentration on only one thing: what the other pilot was doing. Rather than the dozen or more that Drew would be concentrating on. That left part of Amos' mind free for other tasks.

First, he called Jana with an update—enough of a one to get her attention, but not get fire safety after them if they survived this. There were some things that the upper echelons didn't need to know.

"Two hotshots heavy," Amos reported. "Coming out southwest corner. Kinda warm in this here valley. Figgered it was time ta be movin' along." No one on the team had a Texas accent except Jasper—and his wasn't much of one as his folks had moved to Oregon when he was six. Jasper didn't often speak anyway, though more now than before he'd hooked up with Jana—the lucky shit. If Amos lived through this, he was gonna find someone else that hot and maybe do some slowing down himself. Of course he and Drew had been saying that for a long time, but there was such a target-rich field to play in first that it was hard to care.

The "Texan" would alert Jana that when he said "kinda warm" it was way out of the norm.

One kilometer running flat out ahead of the firestorm was fast becoming the longest twenty-five seconds of his life.

Twenty.

Fifteen.

Now it was a pure race between the southern edge of the escarpment and the encroaching smoke and fire.

"Roger that. Y'all just keep your heads down and come home to Mama."

Amos wished he could spare a moment to stare down at the radio in surprise. Jana! Jana didn't speak Texan any more than the rest of them. Woman rarely joked at all.

"Who *are* you people?" The hotshot asked from the rear, but there wasn't time to answer. They'd been flying low—standard put-out-building-fire kind of low—which was far lower than running-like-your-tail-was-on-fire kind of low. Moving this close to the ground at this speed was something they'd only done once or twice in the Army.

*Head down?* So, not good.

Up ahead, Drew took them down another ten feet.

"Yipes!" The hotshot's exclamation was loud enough to hurt despite his headphones.

If he had time, he'd agree.

An instant later, the other four Firebirds raced straight at them in two pairs—thirty feet higher, skimming just below the smoke ceiling, and only two rotors apart. They dumped their loads of water to either side of the escape path, knocking it wider for just a moment.

Amos raced after Drew as they hammered down the center of the momentary opening.

The other four helos would now be pulling max G's to make the turn. He wished he had a ground camera. All six Firebirds, flashing by in a long line just above the ground between two towering pillars of fire about to close. That was a moment to remember.

"By the numbers," Jana called—couldn't the woman at least *sound* worried?

Each of the six of them reported "clear" as they rolled clear from the fire front. It was hard to keep the adrenaline howl of laughter off the air. Sector 39-04 was now a hundred percent on fire, but they were clear.

"Damn that was close," the hotshot leaned forward between the two pilot seats.

Amos glanced over but any words died in his throat. He hadn't so much as seen her face when she dove aboard. Hadn't even connected that the hotshot was female until the second or third yell about her sister. Like the military, the hotshot teams were about twenty percent female and rising slowly. So, one in five that he'd rescue a female. One in twenty-five that they were both women.

He'd thought he was ready for all that. But his momentary glance aside from the path of Drew's flight had revealed her face. Still wearing full hotshot gear, she'd shed her foil shelter and her helmet. She had a long, elegant face framed in sleek brunette hair with light brown eyes that looked as if they were filled with triumph.

"Yeah," he managed, turning his attention back to the flight. "That was close."

# 6

"I swear to god, I had no idea she was a woman."

Amos laughed at his friend's expense plus a little extra to rub it in. They were halfway into dinner. Frank's Diner sat right on the edge of Finnon Lake just two miles from the Swansboro Country Airport where the Firebirds were stationed. The Placerville Airport was crammed with the bigger boys, so they'd been shoved off to the side. Thankfully, Frank's—the only restaurant for ten miles around—served up a fine feed and a cold beer.

"You sure?" Drew wasn't convinced yet.

"You blind, bro? Or was she that homely? Her sister…now that *was* hot."

"Never saw her face," Drew took a thoughtful bite of his double burger.

The guy still had such Upper West Side manners that he finished chewing before he continued the thought that Amos could see he was still in the middle of.

"Didn't speak once that I could hear. Was a little busy flying, you know. Not just trailing along like some baby robin following papa through the sky."

Amos was still hot on the trail of Drew not knowing he'd saved a woman, so he ignored the other dig.

Drew continued, "When we hit the ground, she—guess it could have been a she—said thanks and offered a solid handshake. Most of her face was blocked by the foil shelter she had all bundled up in her arms."

"'Cause she took one look at you, bro, and was afraid her face would melt. Using the shelter to fend you off, worse than fire."

"Just eat your damned chicken fried steak." Drew had never properly appreciated meat wrapped in too much deep-fried breading smothered in rich gravy. It was Amos' idea of heaven. His dad used to make it for him, when there weren't any fashion-model appetites around to appease.

Amos waved some of Frank's Garlicky Fries at Drew. "Telling you, the firefighter in my bird was flaming hot. And she yelled about the other one being her sister—musta been afraid you were gonna weasel out like usual and leave her behind. Can't imagine sisters falling that far apart in hotness."

"Remember the Claricks?"

Amos could only shudder. Drew had met one and set up a half-blind double date to include Amos and her sister. The first had seemed normal enough; the other definitely a coyote date—the kind you would gnaw your arm off to get away from what she passed off as a personality. Crazy town.

"I'm telling you though the one in my bird... freaking amazing."

"Get her name?"

Amos hadn't and was still kicking himself, but he wasn't going to admit it. "Got the name of the babe in yours..." he teased. From her sister screaming it loud enough to knock his helo out of the sky.

"Julie," a voice said from over his right shoulder. "Julie Falcone."

Amos twisted around to see the woman who'd stepped out of the shadows behind their booth. It was the face from his helo. He'd never forget a face like that. And now it wasn't just framed by sweaty and muddy brunette hair, it was framed by a flowing miracle of shiny walnut brown that spilled down to her shoulders. Beautiful had become shocking. Her body, sweetly long and trim, was revealed by a tight red t-shirt from the mid-summer Dundee fire and tight jeans.

"No, Julie was your sister's name. You can't both be named Julie."

"Ha!" Drew laughed. "I knew you didn't get the name of the babe, er, woman in your helo."

"Hi," another Julie double stepped around from behind Julie. "I'm Natalie. I was the 'freaking amazing' one that was in the back of your helo."

He glanced at Drew, "You seeing double, bro?"

"Never been so happy to be," he mumbled softly. Then he jolted to his feet. "Would you ladies care to join us?"

*Damn it!* Drew's recovery time was incredible. Amos rose as well, but he was always a step slower than Drew on manners.

The twins—right down to the t-shirt and buff conditioning—exchanged a glance followed by an infinitesimal shared shrug.

"You saved our lives," Natalie answered for both of them. "That has to make up for your babe-this and hot-that. Some."

"Not all," Julie's look said she was less convinced, but resigned to her fate.

"Yeah, we're really…" Drew started.

"…sorry about that," Amos finished. "But getting to tease my bro about not even noticing he'd rescued a beautiful hotshot was too good a chance to miss."

"Your brother?" Natalie sat beside him, just close enough to smell like the outdoors and that delicious hint of fire smoke that could never be wholly scrubbed away. It was like ambrosia to a firefighter. On a woman as beautiful as Natalie, it was almost overwhelming.

"Well, other than him being from the snooty part of Manhattan…" Amos shrugged.

"…close enough to true," Drew admitted as he made room for Julie. "Though the good Lord knows I've tried to get rid of him."

"He says I'm like a bad Brooklyn rash. He's only jealous because he can't climb out of my shadow. Other than that, we're twins too." Despite his own pasty-white skin in contrast to Drew's clean-shaved dark coloring.

The women exchanged another one of those unreadable looks. Then Julie finally sat next to Drew. Her face ran to more serious expressions; Natalie's lighter nature had almost broken to a laugh. It made her eyes tip just a little more toward golden than her twin's.

# 7

"Your solution to a bad breakup..." Amos looked at her in shock.

"...and losing their jobs..." Drew added in.

"And losing your jobs, was to become hotshots?"

Natalie answered with a nod as her mouth was presently full with a bite of her burger.

"What's next? First twin astronauts in space?"

"There's Mark and Scott Kelly," Julie pointed out.

"Not together," Drew noted.

Natalie liked that both guys simply assumed nothing was out of her and Julie's reach.

"Space..." Julie looked thoughtful.

Natalie worked hard to suppress a laugh. Julie was the master of the double entendre. Her dry tone also said space away from the two guys. They were clearly ladies' men, that had been obvious even without overhearing their earlier conversation. It was also clear that they rated Natalie and her sister as prime targets. And why shouldn't they? She and Julie were hot stuff, even if she did say so herself. Didn't mean she was going to sleep with one of them.

But she couldn't shake off that first look Amos had given her aboard the racing helicopter. Their survival had been in doubt, deep doubt based on the walls of flame visible out his front windshield. She'd been covered in mud and soot, and wearing full hotshot gear. And still, despite the crisis of the moment, he'd stared at her as if he'd seen a magazine centerfold. She and Julie were used to attention when they dressed up to hit a club and went dancing—they'd practiced as dance partners since they could walk and knew how to take over a floor. That wasn't how she'd looked after being dragged out of the fire.

Still, he looked at her that way.

And he and Drew were funny together, though it was clear that Amos was the punchline man of the team. Only rarely did he let Drew finish a sentence, but Drew's reactions also said that Amos rarely got his meaning wrong. It was a different kind of twin-speak than hers and Julie's, which she found intriguing.

"So, did you guys share a womb?"

"Considered it," Amos deadpanned it. "Drew's mom *is* awesome."

"She is," Drew agreed happily. "But imagine the trouble she'd have giving birth to this Jewish white boy from Brooklyn. He's such a whiner. Just didn't seem fair."

"Better than a hoity uptown piece of trash. He thinks he's smarter than me," he leaned forward to warn Julie. "Can you imagine?"

"I let him think he's smarter. His tiny ego needs all

the help it can get." Drew made a point of looking to Julie to keep her included in the conversation.

Not many guys did that. Julie's quiet nature tended to let her fade into the background—which was fine with her sister. But both of these guys kept her involved, kept inviting her to stay engaged in small ways.

"Mrs. Berkowitz says that Amos was a real handful from birth to…"

"Until now! At least that's Mama's version," Amos laughed.

And Natalie found it easy to join in.

The meal slid by easily, very easily. Natalie found her guy-shield defenses lowering. Designed to rebuff the slavering toad, the grabby slime mold, and the inveterate ladies' man, it wasn't fending off the thoughtful guy who hid behind a mask of funny. Also, she'd seen them fly their helicopters like they were extensions of their very being. That didn't come from being a slacker in any way. The self-confidence they had in that area was hard won and fully deserved.

By the time they were leaving, she was idly wondering what other areas they were confident in—with reason. Things had shifted through the meal until there were two separate conversations. Julie and Drew talking about firefighting, spaceflight, and movies. Her own conversation with Amos was filled with enough laughter that her sides were pleasantly sore.

The guys drove an immaculate and testosterone-huge GMC Denali pickup. It had the Firebirds' logo on the door, red-and-orange flames on the hood, and was rigged for towing. It might be a company rig, but it fit them. The Falcone-mobile was a hard-used Subaru

Forester wagon in mud-spattered bronze. It fit her and Julie.

"Is it named Carmine?" Amos looked down at their car.

Natalie laughed. That was usually the first joke out of anyone's mouth who heard their last name. Carmine Falcone—the villain of so many Batman tales—was usually placed as their father or brother. It was one of her tests actually. If a guy didn't get the joke, it was a big caution flag. If he overused it, it was another kind of flag.

Amos had struck a whole new balance by teasing her car.

"It is now." She glanced at Julie for her approval, but Julie wasn't there.

It took her a moment to spot her twin. She and Drew had walked well into the darkness away from the diner and were looking up at the stars together. An black arc was blocked out of the sky by the fire's smoke cloud to the north, but the main view over the quiet water of Finnon Lake was to the south where the rest of the sky glittered.

"Well, that's a first." Julie was very slow about warming up to guys. Sometimes she'd get in a mood, usually on the dance floor. Then her sister would burst out of her shell and shimmy like a sex goddess just to drive the men wild. It was one of the few moves that Natalie couldn't keep up with. But this wasn't that at all. They stood apart, but closer than was usual for Julie. Drew was darkly handsome and very smooth in his speech and manners—and it seemed to be working for him.

She turned back to realize that she was so close to

Amos that she had to look up to see his eyes, barely lit by the neon "Open" sign in the diner's window. Amos had a cheery demeanor that seemed to see the bright side of everything. His rough edges, she realized, were a choice. Not an affectation, but a conscious choice of how he chose to approach the world: *here I am, deal with it.*

The neon sign winked out, plunging them deeper into darkness.

They stood little more than a breath apart. After an evening of chatter and laughter, his silence was echoing and pulled her in. Half a step was all it took. Half a step and they came together.

The comedian was gone. The rough edges gone as he leaned down the few inches to kiss her. Lightly as a question, deep as an answer. One hand on her waist, no longer sore with laughter but warm with anticipation. Another resting lightly on the small of her back forcing a sigh from her by its unexpected gentleness.

It would just be a kiss. She was a hotshot and would be back in the woods tomorrow. He'd be flying who knew where. There was only tonight.

But as the roughed-edged man smoothed out her own edges with such skill—another thing he deserved to be confident about—Natalie wished that there was a chance for more than this one moment.

# 8

"Does it make me a bad man?" Amos asked Drew. He didn't do it over their shared frequency. He'd waited until they were back on the ground, getting fuel for their helos and food for their bellies.

"You mean that you hope this fire never gets a hundred percent contained?"

Amos sighed. It had started with that after-dinner kiss.

"Total bone melter."

"Had one of those myself," Drew agreed.

The next day they'd airlifted the twins out to reinsert with their hotshot team. The day after that, the Firebirds had offered transport to lift the entire team, heli-tack style, to a new section of the fire. Six helos could move three hotshots each. One flight had moved eighteen of the team. Then he and Drew had doubled back to pick up the twins and deliver them to a high ridge near their team from which to do some scouting before they rejoined the others.

They might have lingered for a few minutes. Truth be told, he'd wanted to shut down his helo and take the time then and there to discover just how good Natalie would feel if shed of her fire gear. Because she felt beyond amazing in it as she'd leaned into his kiss hard enough to pin him bonelessly against the door of the MD 520N. It had been a little weird to think of Drew and Julie doing the same not fifty feet away, but not too weird. He didn't know a better man than Drew—they'd both saved each other's lives so many times they'd stopped counting. Even guy-tallies hit their limit sometimes. And if Drew had gotten as good from Julie as he had from Natalie, more power to him.

Drew took another bite of his sandwich. "What are we gonna do about this, Amos?"

"Got me, bro. But we can't let this just slide away and fizzle out."

"Not this scale of heat."

They headed aloft no closer to a solution.

# 9

"Drew," Julie said as they took a thirty-second hydration break from cutting a new fireline.

"Amos," Natalie agreed before capping her bottle and reshouldering her Pulaski fire axe. Her muscles ached and zinged above the steady hum of pain that she'd come to identify with Day Four on a fire. She swallowed a couple of Tylenol with the last swirl of moisture in her mouth. In minutes, the smoke would make it achingly dry once again.

"Hotshots still?" she offered Julie when they shifted over to swamping branches—the arduous task of dragging clear the cuttings made by the sawyers. All of the burnable fuels had to be moved clear of the fireline and placed on the far side of the firebreak, which was thankfully downhill this time. Yesterday, it had to be cleared uphill over a hump. Absolute killer.

"One season enough?" Julie's thoughts echoed her own. It had been interesting, challenging, and hard work. The last didn't bother either of them, but after this one season the first two hadn't really grabbed them.

"Then what?"

That stopped them both long enough to stare at each other for a long thoughtful moment.

Julie glanced upward in a little double motion that said she wasn't merely looking at the overhead smoke.

Space.

They didn't have the degrees for that. Just like their mom and dad—who'd met on a building fire after coming from two different engine companies (as if that wasn't a slightly creepy echo of the current situation)—she and Julie had spent most of their lives in and around fires.

Space. While that might be out of their reach, they could do almost anything else. They'd long ago agreed that neither of them was interested in cashing in on their looks, though they'd had offers from the fashion runway to porn movies. But they were both smart and strong, especially after a season working as hotshots rather than Public Information Officer and interdepartmental liaison as they had back in their dumb-enough-to-date-twins days.

The firefight ran through that night and much of the next day, but they managed to halt the fire in its tracks. Helos and air tankers buzzed overhead. Air commanders above them. A second hotshot team did a set to the west and they held the line. Even the little Firebirds came in from their usual house-saving details to chase spot fires wherever they cropped up.

When the madness finally died down—over forty-eight after they'd arrived on side of the fire and started digging in for the fight—a dozer finally managed to cut a new road into the area. A Category II team rolled in with a trio of wildland fire engines to take over the cleanup. The hotshot team loaded up their gear—axes, saws, fuel, and their few scraps of camp gear—then began the long walk out. Not a one of them weren't stumbling like drunks. It had been two full days on the line with only a two-hour catnap. Dropping off the adrenaline on the fireline left them with almost nothing to get out of these damned woods.

It was a pleasant surprise when less than a mile later, they broke out into the open.

"Pavement," Julie sighed happily.

"Civilization," another hotshot agreed. They stood along the edge of a one-lane road that felt like freedom.

"Cold water," Natalie could barely croak, but it would be near now. She had no idea exactly where they were; glad to just focus on lifting one foot after the next as someone else led them out of the woods.

The sun was setting, blood red in the smoke haze. It was a major improvement now that the fire was dying. They hadn't seen the sun since entering the diner for that first dinner with Drew and Amos.

Nobody was moving.

Maybe they'd just sleep here beside the road.

Then, by some miracle, a set of headlights stabbed through the descending darkness.

Not one, but two heaven-sent Denali pickups rolled up to stop in front of them.

"We heard your team was coming out this way," Amos grinned at her from the driver's seat. Drew sat beside him, his grin was even bigger. She didn't know if she'd ever been as happy to see anyone in her life. The cabins were full with other people, but she was more than happy to pile in the truck bed with the other hotshots.

Once they were loaded, the mood rose fast. Saved the final trudging walk, they'd beaten back the fire. She and Julie leaned shoulder to shoulder and enjoyed the others' laughter and joking. They'd not only beaten back another fire, they'd beaten back a fire *season*. The team would disband and scatter now through the winter months. Those who wanted to, would show up for the next season and bring on another set of rookies—just as she and Julie had been eight months ago.

But another season hotshotting wasn't for them. She didn't know what was, but that wasn't it.

The trucks were moving slowly up the narrow road. She smelled it first. The char—not of burning forest—but of cooking meat. Not burned past recognition—like the occasional deer or other wildlife who hadn't made good their escape from the fire. It smelled like…

"Food!" One of the crowd shouted out.

The trucks pulled into the driveway of a massive three-story house tucked back in the trees. Major bonus! The trees weren't burning.

Amos climbed down and was standing beside the truck bed. "Locals are so glad we all saved their homes, they're throwing us a party. Burgers and dogs on the grill. Hot showers and a swimming pool!" He had to shout the last over the cheers of the team.

Everyone scrambled and jumped down. When she and Julie reached the tail of the bed, Amos and Drew were waiting for them.

"You'll get dirty," she warned them as they reached out to help them down. Two days deep in the smoke, she and Julie were both darker than Drew—soot-black rather than beautiful brown.

"Caring about…"

"…this much." Both men held their thumb and forefinger pinched tightly together.

Her own gasp matched Julie's as they each were grabbed by their waist and set on the ground. Amos' enveloping hug was sweet, but his devouring kiss rang bells all up and down her body. When he finally let her go, she could see the full-body char outline she'd left on his clothes. She pointed at it and he just shrugged happily before snugging her in against his side.

Drew rolled his eyes when he looked down at the matching imprint Julie had left on his own clothes. But he only sighed once before he shrugged and pulled Julie against his hip as well. Natalie had always loved walking arm-in-arm, though it had never been one of Julie's things. This time it didn't look as if she was minding it very much.

They showered, they ate, they belly flopped into the pool. The owners had a big hamper filled with men's swim trunks and various women's suits. After a quick glance consultation with Julie, they'd both selected the skimpiest bikinis they could find. Amos' and Drew's stunned-puppy reactions were well worth the hoots and catcalls from the rest of the team.

## 10

Jana waited and watched. She and her brother had founded the Oregon Firebirds eight months ago. They, along with Curt's best friend Jasper, had spent three years planning—and then gambled everything against this shot at launching a firefighting helicopter team.

It had turned out in ways she'd never imagined despite all of her careful planning.

The fires had burned and the jobs had flowed. They were still a year from being debt-free, maybe two—six helicopters and all of the personnel and support vehicles didn't come cheap. But they were far more cashflow positive than even her most optimistic projections. She'd built in contingencies and negotiated early payment bonuses as much as she could, and it had worked.

But it wasn't only the Oregon Firebirds that had exceeded expectations. The pilots and crew had come together not like fliers, but like family.

Her and Curt's biological family hadn't been much of a one. But the Oregon Firebirds…

Her brother and Stacy now frolicked in the deep end of the pool just like the newlyweds they were.

Palo watched raptly from the pool's edge as Maggie did a dive off the board that was as beautiful as she was.

And her own Jasper was easy to spot in his ever-present cowboy hat. He crossed the deck toward her carrying two fresh beers in one hand and a plate with a pair of enormous brownies in the other. He planted a kiss on the top of her head where she sat upright on a lounger.

He held her beer bottle steady until she had a good grasp on it with the hooks that had replaced her right hand and knocked her out of the sky into being an administrator rather than a pilot. He didn't see her having one arm as any bit of a handicap; he just helped in small, thoughtful ways.

"Good summer," he said softly, his voice tickling her ear as he slid into the lounger behind her and eased her back against his chest.

"Beyond good," she agreed and bit into the brownie. "I've been watching the boys."

Jasper's harrumph of irritation was a tease.

She knew that he knew what she meant.

"Look mighty happy, don't they?" Jasper waved his bottle toward them.

"They do." Drew and Amos were sporting with the twins in the pool. They were playing in a way that could only happen when it meant more than just the physical. There was a care there, an ease that she'd never have been able to see at the start of the season—not until Jasper had helped her discover it in herself.

"Might have heard this hotshot team was done for the season."

"Might have heard that myself," she agreed.

"Might have also heard that those two weren't real anxious to go hotshotting next year."

That she hadn't heard. She'd come to like Natalie and Julie, at least as much as she could in the few moments the boys had spared them for. Over burgers, potato salad, and massive bags of salty chips, they'd talked about past jobs—what they'd liked, what they hadn't.

"They're a fire family to the core."

"Daughters of a chief mother and a lieutenant father," Jana had gotten that from them as well.

"You got some ideas, pretty lady?" Jasper's hand slid around her waist to hold her close.

"Seems I might," his big hand spanned across her belly and made her feel so safe and sure. Sure of herself…and of them. "We've got that contract flying support for burn restoration. Could use some help with coordinating the effort. Field liaison and the like."

Jasper leaned down far enough to nuzzle a kiss against her temple. "That's my kind of Firebird."

And Jana knew that he was no longer talking about the twins. They'd talk more, but she just knew that between them they could make it fly. Drew and Julie. Amos and Natalie. The family would grow a little more and the Firebirds would fly a little higher.

But Jasper was talking about her.

Her wings had been cut when she'd lost her hand in that accident.

But as manager of the Firebirds, as a woman lying in the arms of the man who'd loved her since that first day when he was six and she was ten, she felt as if her wings had regrown. As long as she had these people around her—they could fly forever.

## LAST WORDS

So, you see, as I mentioned much earlier, my story of twins didn't end the way I expected. It's a love story. So, it should end with the lovers…right?

Not according to Jana.

I love the ending she chose (yes it was her, after I'd battered at seven (7!) different ways for the guys to end it). Perhaps even more than her befriending Stacy in the first story or finding her own true love in the third, it is in the last scene of this tale that Jana becomes one of my super heroines that I so love writing.

As to my airborne wildland firefighters, I actually don't know if this is the last word. I had thought that *Wild Fire* had completed all the stories I had to tell in their world, apparently not.

It is one of the peculiar joys of being a writer—I'm never sure what's coming next. Oh, I plan things. As I mentioned, some writers don't, but I know what I want to write next and typically several titles after that.

At least until the next time someone like Jana comes

and sits down next to my writer's chair, daring me to tell their story.

# WILDFIRE AT DAWN (EXCERPT)

## IF YOU LIKED THIS, YOU'LL LOVE THE SMOKEJUMPER NOVELS!

# WILDFIRE AT DAWN

(EXCERPT)

Mount Hood Aviation's lead smokejumper Johnny Akbar Jepps rolled out of his lower bunk careful not to bang his head on the upper. Well, he tried to roll out, but every muscle fought him, making it more a crawl than a roll. He checked the clock on his phone. Late morning.

He'd slept twenty of the last twenty-four hours and his body felt as if he'd spent the entire time in one position. The coarse plank flooring had been worn smooth by thousands of feet hitting exactly this same spot year in and year out for decades. He managed to stand upright...then he felt it, his shoulders and legs screamed.

Oh, right.

The New Tillamook Burn. Just about the nastiest damn blaze he'd fought in a decade of jumping wildfires. Two hundred thousand acres—over three hundred square miles—of rugged Pacific Coast Range forest, poof! The worst forest fire in a decade for the Pacific Northwest, but they'd killed it off without a single fatality or losing a single town. There'd been a few bigger ones, out in the flatter eastern part of Oregon state. But that much area—mostly on terrain too steep to climb even when it wasn't on fire—had been a horror.

Akbar opened the blackout curtain and winced against the summer brightness of blue sky and towering trees that lined the firefighter's camp. Tim was gone from the upper bunk, without kicking Akbar on his way out. He must have been as hazed out as Akbar felt.

He did a couple of side stretches and could feel every single minute of the eight straight days on the wildfire to contain the bastard, then the excruciating nine days more to convince it that it was dead enough to hand off to a Type II incident mop-up crew. Not since his beginning days on a hotshot crew had he spent seventeen days on a single fire.

And in all that time nothing more than catnaps in the acrid safety of the "black"—the burned-over section of a fire, black with char and stark with no hint of green foliage. The mop-up crews would be out there for weeks before it was dead past restarting, but at least it was truly done in. That fire wasn't merely contained; they'd killed it bad.

Yesterday morning, after demobilizing, his team of smokies had pitched into their bunks. No wonder he was so damned sore. His stretches worked out the worst of the kinks but he still must be looking like an old man stumbling about.

He looked down at the sheets. Damn it. They'd been fresh before he went to the fire, now he'd have to wash them again. He'd been too exhausted to shower before sleeping and they were all smeared with the dirt and soot that he could still feel caking his skin. Two-Tall Tim, his number two man and as tall as two of Akbar, kinda, wasn't in his bunk. His towel was missing from the hook.

Shower. Shower would be good. He grabbed his own towel and headed down the dark, narrow hall to the far end of the bunk house. Every one of the dozen doors of his smoke teams were still closed, smokies still sacked out. A glance down another corridor and he could see that at least a couple of the Mount Hood Aviation helicopter crews were up, but most still had closed doors with no hint of light from open curtains sliding under them. All of MHA had gone above and beyond on this one.

"Hey, Tim." Sure enough, the tall Eurasian was in one of the shower stalls, propped up against the back wall letting the hot water stream over him.

"Akbar the Great lives," Two-Tall sounded half asleep.

"Mostly. Doghouse?" Akbar stripped down and hit the next stall. The old plywood dividers were flimsy with age and gray with too many showers. The Mount Hood Aviation firefighters' Hoodie One base camp had been a kids' summer camp for decades. Long since defunct, MHA had taken it over and converted the playfields into landing areas for their helicopters, and regraded the main road into a decent airstrip for the spotter and jump planes.

"Doghouse? Hell, yeah. I'm like ten thousand calories short." Two-Tall found some energy in his voice at the idea of a trip into town.

The Doghouse Inn was in the nearest town. Hood River lay about a half hour down the mountain and had exactly what they needed: smokejumper-sized portions and a very high ratio of awesomely fit young women come to windsurf the Columbia Gorge. The Gorge, which formed the Washington and Oregon border, provided a fantastically target-rich environment for a smokejumper too long in the woods.

"You're too tall to be short of anything," Akbar knew he was being a little slow to reply, but he'd only been awake for minutes.

"You're like a hundred thousand calories short of being even a halfway decent size," Tim was obviously recovering faster than he was.

"Just because my parents loved me instead of tying me to a rack every night ain't my problem, buddy."

He scrubbed and soaped and scrubbed some more until he felt mostly clean.

"I'm telling you, Two-Tall. Whoever invented the hot shower, that's the dude we should give the Nobel prize to."

"You say that every time."

"You arguing?"

He heard Tim give a satisfied groan as some muscle finally let go under the steamy hot water. "Not for a second."

Akbar stepped out and walked over to the line of sinks, smearing a hand back and forth to wipe the condensation from the sheet of stainless steel screwed to the wall. His hazy reflection still sported several smears of char.

"You so purdy, Akbar."

"Purdier than you, Two-Tall." He headed back into the shower to get the last of it.

"So not. You're jealous."

Akbar wasn't the least bit jealous. Yes, despite his lean height, Tim was handsome enough to sweep up any ladies he wanted.

But on his own, Akbar did pretty damn well himself. What he didn't have in height, he made up for with a proper smokejumper's muscled build. Mixed with his tan-dark Indian complexion, he did fine.

The real fun, of course, was when the two of them went cruising together. The women never knew what to make of the two of them side by side. The contrast kept them off balance enough to open even more doors.

He smiled as he toweled down. It also didn't hurt that their opening answer to "what do you do" was "I jump out of planes to fight forest fires."

Worked every damn time. God he loved this job.

---

The small town of Hood River, a winding half-an-hour down the mountain from the MHA base camp, was hopping. Mid-June, colleges letting out. Students and the younger set of professors high-tailing it to the Gorge. They packed the bars and breweries and sidewalk cafes. Suddenly every other car on the street had a windsurfing board tied on the roof.

The snooty rich folks were up at the historic Timberline Lodge on Mount Hood itself, not far in the other direction from MHA. Down here it was a younger, thrill seeker set and you could feel the energy.

There were other restaurants in town that might have better pickings, but the Doghouse Inn was MHA tradition and it was a good luck charm—no smokie in his right mind messed with that. This was the bar where all of the MHA crew hung out. It didn't look like much from the outside, just a worn old brick building beaten by the Gorge's violent weather. Aged before its time, which had been long ago.

But inside was awesome. A long wooden bar stretched down one side with a half-jillion microbrew taps and a small but well-stocked kitchen at the far end. The dark wood paneling, even on the ceiling, was barely visible beneath thousands of pictures of doghouses sent from patrons all over the world. Miniature dachshunds in ornately decorated shoeboxes, massive Newfoundlands in backyard mansions that could easily house hundreds of their smaller kin, and everything in between. A gigantic Snoopy atop his doghouse in full Red Baron fighting gear dominated the far wall. Rumor said Shulz himself had been here two owners before and drawn it.

Tables were grouped close together, some for standing and drinking, others for sitting and eating.

"Amy, sweetheart!" Two-Tall called out as they entered the bar. The perky redhead came out from behind the bar to receive a hug from Tim. Akbar got one in turn, so he wasn't complaining. Cute as could be and about his height; her hugs were better than taking most women to bed. Of course, Gerald the cook and the bar's co-owner was big enough and strong enough to squish either Tim or Akbar if they got even a tiny step out of line with his wife. Gerald was one amazingly lucky man.

Akbar grabbed a Walking Man stout and turned to assess the crowd. A couple of the air jocks were in. Carly and Steve were at a little table for two in the corner, obviously not interested in anyone's company but each others. Damn, that had happened fast. New guy on the base swept up one of the most beautiful women on the planet. One of these days he'd have to ask Steve how he'd done that. Or maybe not. It looked like they were settling in for the long haul; the big "M" was so not his own first choice.

Carly was also one of the best FBANs in the business. Akbar was a good Fire Behavior Analyst, had to be or he wouldn't have made it to first stick—lead smokie of the whole MHA crew. But Carly was something else again. He'd always found the Flame Witch, as she was often called, daunting and a bit scary besides; she knew the fire better than it did itself. Steve had latched on to one seriously driven lady. More power to him.

The selection of female tourists was especially good today, but no other smokies in yet. They'd be in soon enough…most of them had groaned awake and said they were coming as he and Two-Tall kicked their hallway doors, but not until they'd been on their way out—he and Tim had first pick. Actually some of the smokies were coming, others had told them quite succinctly where they could go—but hey, jumping into fiery hell is what they did for a living anyway, so no big change there.

A couple of the chopper pilots had nailed down a big table right in the middle of the bustling seating area: Jeannie, Mickey, and Vern. Good "field of fire" in the immediate area.

He and Tim headed over, but Akbar managed to snag the chair closest to the really hot lady with down-her-back curling dark-auburn hair at the next table over—set just right to see her profile easily. Hard shot, sitting there with her parents, but damn she was amazing. And if that was her mom, it said the woman would be good looking for a long time to come.

Two-Tall grimaced at him and Akbar offered him a comfortable "beat out your ass" grin. But this one didn't feel like that. Maybe it was the whole parental thing. He sat back and kept his mouth shut.

He made sure that Two-Tall could see his interest. That made Tim honor bound to try and cut Akbar out of the running.

---

Laura Jenson had spotted them coming into the restaurant. Her dad was only moments behind.

"Those two are walking like they just climbed off their first-ever horseback ride."

She had to laugh, they did. So stiff and awkward they barely managed to move upright. They didn't look like first-time windsurfers, aching from the unexpected workout. They'd also walked in like they thought they were two gifts to god, which was even funnier. She turned away to avoid laughing in their faces. Guys who thought like that rarely appreciated getting a reality check.

*Available at fine retailers everywhere.*

## ABOUT THE AUTHOR

M.L. Buchman started the first of over 60 novels, 100 short stories, and a fast-growing pile of audiobooks while flying from South Korea to ride his bicycle across the Australian Outback. Part of a solo around the world trip that ultimately launched his writing career in: thrillers, military romantic suspense, contemporary romance, and SF/F.

Recently named in *The 20 Best Romantic Suspense Novels: Modern Masterpieces* by ALA's Booklist, they have also selected his works three times as "Top-10 Romance Novel of the Year." His thrillers have been praised noting, "Tom Clancy fans will clamor for more."

As a 30-year project manager with a geophysics degree who has: designed and built houses, flown and jumped out of planes, and solo-sailed a 50' ketch, he is awed by what's possible. More at: www.mlbuchman.com.

# Other works by M. L. Buchman: *(\* - also in audio)*

## Thrillers

### Dead Chef
Swap Out!
One Chef!
Two Chef!

### Miranda Chase
Drone*
Thunderbolt*
Condor*

## Romantic Suspense

### Delta Force
Target Engaged*
Heart Strike*
Wild Justice*
Midnight Trust*

### Firehawks
**Main Flight**
Pure Heat
Full Blaze
Hot Point*
Flash of Fire*
Wild Fire

**Smokejumpers**
Wildfire at Dawn*
Wildfire at Larch Creek*
Wildfire on the Skagit*

### The Night Stalkers
**Main Flight**
The Night Is Mine
I Own the Dawn
Wait Until Dark
Take Over at Midnight
Light Up the Night
Bring On the Dusk
By Break of Day

**and the Navy**
Christmas at Steel Beach
Christmas at Peleliu Cove

**White House Holiday**
Daniel's Christmas*
Frank's Independence Day*
Peter's Christmas*
Zachary's Christmas*
Roy's Independence Day*
Damien's Christmas*

**5E**
Target of the Heart
Target Lock on Love
Target of Mine
Target of One's Own

### Shadow Force: Psi
At the Slightest Sound*
At the Quietest Word*

### White House Protection Force
Off the Leash*
On Your Mark*
In the Weeds*

## Contemporary Romance

### Eagle Cove
Return to Eagle Cove
Recipe for Eagle Cove
Longing for Eagle Cove
Keepsake for Eagle Cove

### Henderson's Ranch
Nathan's Big Sky*
Big Sky, Loyal Heart*
Big Sky Dog Whisperer*

### Love Abroad
Heart of the Cotswolds: England
Path of Love: Cinque Terre, Italy

## Other works by M. L. Buchman:

### Contemporary Romance (cont)

**Where Dreams**
*Where Dreams are Born*
*Where Dreams Reside*
*Where Dreams Are of Christmas*
*Where Dreams Unfold*
*Where Dreams Are Written*

### Science Fiction / Fantasy

**Deities Anonymous**
*Cookbook from Hell: Reheated*
*Saviors 101*

**Single Titles**
*The Nara Reaction*
*Monk's Maze*
*the Me and Elsie Chronicles*

### Non-Fiction

**Strategies for Success**
*Managing Your Inner Artist/Writer*
*Estate Planning for Authors\**
*Character Voice*
*Narrate and Record Your Own Audiobook\**

## Short Story Series by M. L. Buchman:

### Romantic Suspense

**Delta Force**
*Delta Force*

**Firehawks**
*The Firehawks Lookouts*
*The Firehawks Hotshots*
*The Firebirds*

**The Night Stalkers**
*The Night Stalkers*
*The Night Stalkers 5E*
*The Night Stalkers CSAR*
*The Night Stalkers Wedding Stories*

**US Coast Guard**
*US Coast Guard*

**White House Protection Force**
*White House Protection Force*

### Contemporary Romance

**Eagle Cove**
*Eagle Cove*

**Henderson's Ranch**
*Henderson's Ranch\**

**Where Dreams**
*Where Dreams*

### Thrillers

**Dead Chef**
*Dead Chef*

### Science Fiction / Fantasy

**Deities Anonymous**
*Deities Anonymous*

**Other**
*The Future Night Stalkers*
*Single Titles*

SIGN UP FOR M. L. BUCHMAN'S
NEWSLETTER TODAY

*and receive:*
***Release News***
***Free Short Stories***
***a Free Book***

***Do it today. Do it now.***
***http://free-book.mlbuchman.com***